A drop of water slowly wound its way down Jack's chest

When it finally disappeared beneath the waistband of his sweatpants, Corie's mouth went dry. She was suddenly aware of his scent—sunshine, sweat and something very male. She tried to turn her eyes away, to gather her thoughts. But it was useless.

"What are you doing here?" Jack asked.

Staring. That's what she was doing, and her imagination kicked into overdrive, picturing what might happen if she had the courage to go to him now and with her hand, her tongue, follow the path that drop of water had taken.

"I thought…" In a minute she'd be able to speak coherently. But first she had to get her eyes off the waistband of his pants. Dragging her gaze up to meet his, she said, "You said we'd talk in the morning."

"Talk. Yeah. What do you want to talk about?" he asked awkwardly.

Narrowing her gaze, Corie studied Jack, and for the first time noticed that he looked a little dazed. Could he possibly be feeling even a fraction of what she was experiencing? The possibility gave her courage. *Tell the man what you want.* Her friend's words became a chant in her head.

Corie cleared her throat. "Well, I was thinking… I'd like to have hot, wild sex with you."

Dear Reader,

Being a part of Temptation's SINGLE IN THE CITY miniseries has been such fun. First the *man-magnet skirt* took Manhattan, and now it's causing havoc in one of the most romantic cities in the world— San Francisco.

Small-town librarian Corie Benjamin wants to change her life! All she has to do is give in to temptation.

Temptation #1—Jack Kincaid's offer to fly her to San Francisco. If she goes, she can kill two birds with one stone. She can meet the man Jack claims is her father and find out why her mother lied about his death, and she can turn herself into a whole new woman.

Temptation #2—a *man-magnet skirt*. Wearing it will supposedly increase her ability to attract men. Corie figures it's just the ticket she needs to get everything she's looking for.

Temptation #3—Jack Kincaid, who is exactly what she's looking for, the perfect man to have a fling with in San Francisco.

How can a girl possibly say no?

I hope you have fun watching Jack and Corie struggle against temptation and their hearts' desires. And if you want to discover how the *man-magnet skirt* got its start, visit eHarlequin.com and read my online story *Single in San Francisco*. For contests and excerpts of my upcoming books, visit carasummers.com and singleinthecity.org.

Happy reading,

Cara Summers

Cara Summers
FLIRTING WITH TEMPTATION

HARLEQUIN®

TORONTO • NEW YORK • LONDON
AMSTERDAM • PARIS • SYDNEY • HAMBURG
STOCKHOLM • ATHENS • TOKYO • MILAN • MADRID
PRAGUE • WARSAW • BUDAPEST • AUCKLAND

To Heather MacAllister and Kristin Gabriel,
my two writing cohorts in this Single in the City adventure.
I have learned so much from working with the two of you.
Thanks for the inspiration and the fun!

ISBN 0-373-69136-X

FLIRTING WITH TEMPTATION

Copyright © 2003 by Carolyn Hanlon.

Visit us at www.eHarlequin.com

Printed in U.S.A.

Prologue

Dear Mrs. H,
Spectacular! That's the only word that I can think of to describe your wedding photos. Green was the perfect choice for the bridesmaids' dresses. But then our tastes always did coincide.

My research for my screenplay is going well. The two young women who have rented my apartment on a time-share basis are giving me lots of ideas. I've lent the man-magnet skirt to each of them, and the "adventure has begun"! The skirt hasn't lost a bit of its power since you gave it to me. You wouldn't believe some of the male visitors these two women have—from hunky construction workers to alien-abductee investigators. I kid you not! And I thought I'd seen everything while I was living in Manhattan.

I've already accumulated copious notes. The path of true love never runs smoothly—even when it has a little help from a man-magnet skirt.

As I mentioned in my last letter, I've had a devil of a time finding a third tenant, thanks to all the construction work on the other buildings on the block. And I do need the money. With any luck my old college roommate, Jack Kincaid, will come through for me. He has a line on a third young woman—a college librarian from Fairview, Ohio. If he can convince her to fly out here, I may have my best research subject yet. Her story has the potential for an Oscar-winning screenplay—murder, mayhem, old secrets from the past and, of course, true love.

More later. Give my best to Pierre—and to Cleo and Antoine and their new litter of puppies. And let them know that the urban legend of the skirt is living on in San Francisco!

Ta!

Franco Rossi

1

SAN FRANCISCO, HERE I COME...

As she pulled her car into her driveway, Corie Benjamin tried to ignore the little tune that had been playing in her head all day. The moment she turned off the ignition, her gaze strayed to the overnight delivery envelope on the passenger seat. Inside was a plane ticket to San Francisco. Even though she hadn't yet agreed to use it, Jack Kincaid had still sent it to her. The man knew how to tempt a woman.

She picked up the envelope and traced her finger along his name on the return address. The first time she'd heard from him, he'd left a message on her answering machine, telling her his name and how to reach him at the *San Francisco Chronicle.* Of course, none of the details had registered until she'd replayed the message. The first time she'd listened to it, she'd been totally absorbed in his voice. Soft velvet with sandpapery edges was the only way she could describe it, and each time she heard it, a tingle of awareness went right through her. She'd called him back, and what he'd told her had set her head spinning. If she would fly to San Francisco, he would help her meet her father.

Her father. Jack Kincaid couldn't have said anything that would tempt her more. All her life she'd wondered about the man her mother would never speak of. Was she like him? Was he the reason she felt so...restless, so unsatisfied with her life in Fairview, Ohio? She tightened her grip on the envelope, and, for the first time, she understood how Eve must have felt in the Garden of Eden—irresistibly drawn by the promise of knowledge.

But knowledge could be dangerous, she reminded herself as she hugged the envelope to her chest. She might not like the answers she would find.

And she had obligations at the library. Dropping everything and flying off to San Francisco would be irresponsible…and wild…and wonderful…

"Never act on impulse." In her mind, Corie could hear her mother reciting her most frequently repeated commandment as clearly as if she were sitting right next to her in the car. The first time Isabella Benjamin had said those words, Corie had been six. After reading *Peter Pan* for the first time, she'd climbed onto the roof of the house and tried to fly. Six weeks in bed with a broken leg had given her ample opportunity to reflect on the virtue of being cautious. Not that she'd learned her lesson. Being cautious just didn't seem to be part of her nature. She had to work at it constantly.

A glance at her watch had her slipping out of the car and racing up the flagstone path. In less than fifteen minutes, Jack Kincaid was going to call and ask if she was going to use the ticket. The moment of decision was upon her.

"Yoo-hoo! Corie!"

Busted, Corie thought as she hit the top step of the porch and turned. "Afternoon, Ms. Ponsonby."

Since Corie's mother had died two months ago, Muriel Ponsonby, Fairview, Ohio's town crier, had made it her mission in life to watch over Corie.

"You're home early." Eyes narrowing, Muriel moved to the steps of her porch. "You feeling all right?"

Corie beamed a smile at Muriel. "I'm fine. It's such a lovely day, I just decided to leave work early."

Muriel frowned. "You'll make bridge club tonight?"

"Wouldn't miss it." Muriel had seen to it that Corie had been invited to take her mother's place in the bridge club, the quilting circle and the Friday evening book-discussion group. Corie tightened her grip on the airline ticket. If she stayed in Fairview, her life was all safely mapped out for her. She would turn into her mother.

"Heard you got an overnight delivery letter at the library today. From San Francisco. Not bad news, I hope."

Corie had often thought that the U.S. government should have the kind of spy network that Muriel seemed to have in place. For one wild moment she was tempted to wave the envelope and say, "Just a little note from a lover I met on the Internet. I'm going to fly out and meet him on Wednesday."

But if she did that, Muriel and the entire quilting circle would probably rush to her house to do an intervention. Ever since her failed attempt to fly off the roof, she'd had a reputation for acting recklessly, and in Fairview a reputation *stuck*.

Stifling the impulse to mention an Internet lover or any other kind, Corie backed toward her door, but she couldn't resist saying, "It's just an article I ordered for Dean Atwell—something on poisonous mushrooms."

"Poisonous mushrooms?" Muriel said, looking for all the world like a dog picking up a new scent. "Why would he want something like that?"

Muriel didn't seem to expect an answer. She was too busy backing toward her own front door. In a few minutes, the phone lines would be buzzing since everyone in town knew that Dean Atwell's divorce was not going well. Any twinge of conscience that Corie might have felt at her lie was eased when she pushed her key into the lock and escaped into her house. She'd come home early to gather her thoughts. A quick glance at her watch told her that she now had less than ten minutes to finalize her decision.

To go to San Francisco or not to go—that was the question. Placing the ticket on the small table next to the phone, Corie sank down into a straight-backed chair and fished her notebook out of her bag. From the time she'd been a little girl, doodling had always helped her to see things more clearly. Quickly, she sketched a huge Y. It was the same one she'd been drawing at the library all week. Following the right-hand prong of the Y would keep her trapped safely in her present cocoon as a college librarian in Fairview, Ohio, population eight thousand and dropping. She drew a little circle to represent a cocoon at the end of that path. Following the other path would offer her the chance to escape. To become a butterfly. Quickly, she sketched wings at the end of the left-hand prong. More important, she would get the opportunity to meet the man who could very well be her father and perhaps discover why her mother had kept his existence a secret all these years. Maybe she could figure out why she couldn't be happy with the life her mother had chosen. And maybe, just maybe, she could figure out who she really was.

Just the thought of that had a mix of anticipation and fear forming a tight, hard knot in her stomach. Placing her notebook on the table, she reached out and ran a finger down the envelope that contained the ticket. The choice should have been a no-brainer, and it would have been if it weren't for the promise she'd made over and over again to her mother.

Shifting her glance, Corie met the eyes of the woman in the small ivory-framed picture next to the phone. Her mother's eyes were so serious, her mouth just hinting at a frown. Isabella Benjamin had worn the same expression on her deathbed and she'd made Corie promise one last time...

Drawing in a deep breath, Corie said, "I know I promised you that I would never leave Fairview."

Deathbed promises should be binding, but it wasn't fair. She would have promised her mother anything during those last days. The illness had come so suddenly, a bad cold that had spread to the lungs, and by the time the doctors had tried to treat it with antibiotics, it was too late. Corie touched her mother's face in the picture. "I want to fly to San Francisco on Wednesday."

Though silence filled the hallway, Corie could hear the echoes of old arguments in her mind. Ever since she could remember, she'd wanted to leave Fairview, to see the world. Her mother had always argued against it. *You're much too impulsive to be on your own.* She did have a tendency to leap before she looked—and the leaps often ended in disaster. There was the time she'd climbed a tree to rescue a cat, and the fire department had had to come for both of them. Of course, she hadn't leapt that time; clearly, she'd learned her lesson that she wasn't Peter Pan. Corie sighed and doodled some more. The biggest disagreement she'd ever had with her mother had been when she'd wanted to go away to college. In the end they'd compromised. She'd gotten to go to Ohio State, but she'd had to live at home and ride the bus to classes. And she'd had to promise to take a job at the small liberal arts college in Fairview when she graduated.

As she studied her mother's picture, Corie felt the familiar wave of frustration and love move through her. "I'm not like you." Not yet.

"I know a promise is a promise. But you lied to me about my father." There she'd said it out loud. "You told me my father was dead." And there was a very good chance that he was alive and kicking—running a very successful winery and health spa in the Napa Valley. She glanced at the cluster of stick figures she'd also drawn at the left-hand end of the *Y*. If Benjamin Lewis *was* her father, she had other family, too—two half-bothers and an Uncle Buddy. She'd done as much research as she could on them. Then with her pencil, she retraced the other stick figure she'd drawn a short distance from the cluster. If she flew out to San Francisco, she would also get to meet Jack Kincaid.

In the past two weeks, she'd done research on him, too. Currently, he was writing feature articles for the *San Francisco Chronicle*. Before that, he'd spent eight years working his way up through various news services by covering hot spots throughout the world, and he'd written a Pulitzer prize-winning book based on his experiences. After pulling it out of her bag, she set it on the table next to her mother's picture. She'd read every word of it, and it had held her spellbound. He'd traveled to all the places that she'd only dreamed about.

Drawing in a deep breath, Corie shifted her gaze back to her mother's picture. "It's not like I'm acting on impulse. I've given the idea some careful thought, and I think we should work out a compromise. I'll spend one week in San Francisco, and then I'll come back." She tried to tell herself that she wouldn't be breaking her promise, just bending it.

The silence that greeted her proposal nearly deafened her. Then the shrill ring of the phone made her jump.

Corie glanced at her watch. She still had five minutes. She *needed* five more minutes.

The phone rang again. The number on the caller ID box told her it was Jack Kincaid. She had to pick it up. What in the world was the matter with her? Was she as afraid of the world as her mother had been? She grabbed the receiver. "Hello."

"Corie, did you get the ticket?"

"Yes."

"Good. You'll leave Columbus at 7:15 a.m. on Wednesday, the day after tomorrow, change planes in Chicago, and touch down in San Francisco shortly before noon."

As Jack spoke, Corie tried to resist the effect that his deep, baritone voice always had on her, but the tingle of awareness began to slide through her.

"I've found you a place to stay. The owner of my building, Franco Rossi, was my roommate in college, and he has an apartment you can use. Two other women are using it on a time-share basis, but it's all yours for the time being. And if you decide to stay on in San Francisco, he's sure that you can work something out with them."

Corie closed her eyes as the tingle reached her toes and she felt them curl.

"How does that sound?"

"Perfect." And Jack Kincaid was almost perfect, too. Opening her eyes, she turned his book over and studied his picture on the jacket. Besides the voice that she was sure could charm snakes, he had dark, unruly hair, the darkest gray eyes she'd ever seen and a dimple in his chin that tempted her to touch it. Unable to resist, Corie ran her finger over it. He was making things so easy for her.

Another of her mother's commandments had been "Never trust a charming man. He'll lie to you and you'll believe him."

Corie suppressed a sigh. Jack Kincaid had already lied to her—or at least lied by omission. Not once during their conversations had he ever told her that the man who might very well be her father had at one time been connected to an organized crime family in New Jersey. Of course, Benjamin Lewis's businesses were supposedly on the up-and-up now. Indeed, according to Jack, he'd become a pillar of the community. On Friday he was going to be honored for building the new children's wing at San Francisco Memorial Hospital.

"Then I'll pick you up at the airport Wednesday morning?" Jack asked.

Corie's gaze slipped to her mother's picture. "I didn't agree to come yet."

There was a moment of silence on the other end of the line. Corie closed her eyes and drew in a deep breath. What was the matter with her? She wouldn't blame him if he gave up on her entirely.

"Corie, you are a very tough sell."

She opened her eyes in surprise. It wasn't anger or impatience she heard in his voice. It was patient amusement.

"The problem is if you don't come, you'll never know if Benjamin Lewis is really your father. Can you live with that question nagging at you for the rest of your life?"

The man sure knew how to hit the nail right on the head. If she didn't go, she'd always wonder about the man who might be her father, wonder what he was like, wonder if she was like him...

A knock at the door had her whirling around. She spotted Muriel Ponsonby through the glass, and, for one brief moment, she was tempted to duck under the table and hide. Too late. Muriel was already waving at her.

"Hold on a minute," she said to Jack. "Someone's at the door." She no sooner pulled it open than Muriel beamed a huge smile at her and said, "Missy La Rue had to cancel for bridge tonight, and Harold Mitzenfeld has agreed to fill in. I'm going to make sure he's your partner."

For a moment, Corie was sorely tempted to fake a faint. It couldn't be all that difficult. All she would have to do was close her eyes and slip bonelessly to the floor. Then Muriel would have to find someone else to be Harold's bridge partner. Middle-aged and portly, Harold Mitzenfeld was a recently widowed geology professor at the college. The few times she'd run into him in the library, his conversation hadn't strayed beyond rocks.

"You're speechless," Muriel said, rubbing her hand together. "I knew you would be. I just had to let you know. Eligible bachelors are so hard to come by in Fairview, but I know your mother would expect me to do my best for you. And she would have approved of Harold. Now, don't you be late." With a wave, Muriel turned and hurried off.

Corie stared after her, but she wasn't seeing Muriel. All she could see was her life in Fairview unfolding before her—an endless sea of bridge clubs, quilting circles, book discussion groups...and Harold Metzenfeld!

Whirling, she closed the door and marched back to the hall table. Jack's face smiled up at her from the book jacket—pure temptation. Then she met her mother's steady gaze—pure guilt trip.

In desperation, she glanced up at the mirror that filled the wall above the table. The person staring back at her did not look like she belonged in San Francisco. Plain brownish blond hair was slipping out of the bun she wore it in. Even at twenty-five, she looked to be exactly what she was—a plain-looking, boring college librarian. In short, she was the kind of woman that her neighbors thought was a perfect match for Harold Metzenfeld.

She did not want to be that woman!

Panic and frustration bubbled up inside of her. She'd felt just this way the day that she'd stood on the roof and wanted so much to fly. She did not want to be Corie Benjamin, drab librarian. And if she went to San Francisco, for seven whole days, she could try her wings and *be* someone else.

Grabbing the phone, she drew in a deep breath and said, "All right. Yes." The moment the words were out, she felt her knees give out and she sank onto the nearest chair.

"Yes, you'll come?" Jack Kincaid asked slowly.

Corie drew in a deep breath. It had to be easier to say the second time. "Yes. I'll catch the seven-fifteen flight on Wednesday."

"That's great. I'll meet you at the airport in the baggage claim area. I'm going to bring a friend with me. You won't be able to miss him. He has very odd taste in clothes."

Clothes! Corie's eyes widened. If she was going to be someone totally different, she was going to need some new ones. And her hair—it was going to need some work too. "I just have one request. You said you'd do anything to help me make this decision."

"Yes?"

"Before I make contact with...Mr. Lewis, I'd like a makeover."

There was a beat of silence on the other end of the line. "A makeover?"

"Yes." She very nearly smiled. It was the very first time she'd heard surprise in Jack Kincaid's voice. "I'm sure you've seen them on TV—on *Oprah*? They take someone fairly...drab and ordinary and completely redo her hair, makeup and clothes. I'll pay for it, of course. I just want to look my best if I'm going to meet my new family."

"A makeover," Jack repeated. "I'll look into it. I'm sure it won't be a problem. Anything else?"

Corie narrowed her eyes as she stared once more at her reflection in the mirror. Was it her imagination or did she look different already? There was certainly a touch more color in her cheeks. And her eyes were brighter.

"No."

"Good. You won't regret this, Corie. I think you'll find the evidence I've gathered very compelling."

Corie sat right where she was for a few minutes after Jack broke the connection. In the two weeks since he'd contacted her, informed her of his theory and set her life spinning, she'd searched the house for some clue that what Jack had told her might be true, and she'd uncovered some compelling evidence of her own. Rising, she now went to the closet and pulled the box down from the shelf. She'd found it under a loose floorboard in her mother's bedroom.

Removing the lid, she picked up the brown envelope and drew out her birth certificate. On it, her father's name was Lewis Benjamin. Not Benjamin Lewis, but it was very suggestive. Replacing it in the envelope, she stared down at the bundles of letters. They'd been written over a period of twenty-six years and they chronicled every important event in her life. There were photos of everything—from her first bath to her first date. There was even a picture of the birthmark on her right arm—the one that her mother had always said was a mark of her heritage. The envelopes were stampless and unsealed. The letters were all written by her mother and addressed to a man named Benjamin Lewis. But they'd never been mailed. The "Benny Letters" was what she'd dubbed them since they'd all begun with "Dear Benny."

Was Benjamin Lewis the charming man who'd lied to her mother? Corie suspected that he was. And that was just the first of many questions. If Benny was her father, why had her mother run away? Corie had only had to read the letters to know that her mother had loved the man she was writing to, so why hadn't Isabella mailed them? And why had she kept "Benny's" existence a secret?

Reaching beneath one of the packets of letters, Corie drew out the only other item in the box, a menu from Edie's Diner, a restaurant in the same town that the Lewis Winery was located in. By calling directory assistance, she'd learned that the diner no longer existed. But when she contacted the chamber of commerce, they'd informed her that Edie's place was now called the Saratoga Grill. She hadn't called, but she intended to go there in person. Perhaps someone could tell her more about her mother.

As she closed the box, Corie wished it were just as simple to put a lid on the feelings rushing through her. Tomorrow she would take the first step on a journey that could lead her to her lifelong dream of having a real family. Tomorrow was the beginning of a whole new life— even though it might only last a week.

So why did she feel so...guilty? Placing the box back in the closet, she walked down the hall to the kitchen, passing by the living room she and her mother had used only on holidays and the dining room table that had never been set for company. How many years had she waited, hoping to break free of this house?

If her mother hadn't died so suddenly two months ago, she might never have been able to leave. She might never have found out that she had a father and a family outside of Fairview. Instead, she might have ended up married to Harold Metzenfeld. Corie shuddered at the thought. Then she glanced at her reflection in the hallway mirror and shuddered again. Maybe she wasn't that woman who was staring back at her. Didn't she deserve the chance to find out?

And she wanted to find out the answers to her questions. She was enough of a realist to know that she might not like the answers. But she owed it to herself to find out why her mother had spent so much of her life as a recluse—and why she wanted Corie to do the same thing.

She'd made the right decision.

If only she could get rid of the nagging voice in the back of her mind that was chanting her mother's third commandment: *Be careful what you wish for.*

JACK ROUNDED THE CORNER, drew in a deep breath, and steeled himself for the final sprint that would take him to the end of Pier 39. At 6:00 a.m. the Fisherman's Wharf area of San Francisco was one of his favorite spots. Later the stores and walkways would be thronged with people. Boats would be blowing their whistles, announcing departures to Sausalito or Alcatraz, and there would be ample evidence that only Disney World and Disneyland surpassed Fisherman's Wharf as a tourist attraction.

But right now, there was silence except for the occasional sharp call of a seagull. Sprinting up a flight of wooden steps, Jack welcomed the burn in his shins and lungs. This morning he'd doubled the length of his run, hoping to ease his tension, but so far it hadn't worked.

He should be feeling relieved and elated that he'd persuaded Corie Benjamin to come to San Francisco today. Instead, he'd spent two sleepless nights, and even now he had that anxious feeling deep in his gut, the one he always had when he was pursuing a lead and something was about to go wrong.

The moment the end of the pier came into view, Jack began to slow his pace. Sun glared off the water, and cars streamed steadily across the Golden Gate Bridge in the distance. "San Francisco at its best," his Aunt Mel would have said.

Just thinking about his aunt had his lips curving. He'd been five when his parents had died in a car crash. His father's sister, Melanie Kincaid, had been in the navy at the time, and it had taken her six months to free herself up to take him in. The months in foster homes had given him the worst memories of his life. His years with his Aunt Mel had given him the best.

"We're the last of the Kincaids, kid," she'd said. "We've got to stick together." And stick they had—until he'd gone away to college.

"Why in hell would you want to go a whole continent away? What's New York got that you can't find right here in San Francisco?"

Everything, Jack thought. Or at least that's what he'd thought at the time. His smile faded as he reached the end of the pier and planted his hands against the railing. He hadn't come here today to rekindle old feelings of guilt. He'd come here because he needed his aunt's advice, and he always felt close to her here.

He glanced at the rows of shops and restaurants. She'd brought him here to celebrate every good report card he'd ever gotten. Since her disappearance twelve years ago, he'd come here whenever his work schedule permitted. Dropping his gaze, Jack watched the dark water swell and push against the pilings. "I was right to talk her into coming out here, Aunt Mel."

Corie Benjamin was his ticket to finding out what had really happened to his aunt when she'd disappeared twelve years ago. He'd been sure then, and he was sure now, that Benny Lewis had been behind his aunt's disappearance. Melanie Kincaid had been working as the Lewis family's personal chef, and she'd discovered something about the family that disturbed her. She wouldn't tell him what, only that she was going to check it out. Later he'd learned that she'd disappeared within hours of calling him that day.

If only he'd been closer, he might have...

Impatiently, Jack pushed the thought away. Wallowing in guilt wouldn't change the fact that he'd been a whole continent away, and by the time he'd made it back to San Francisco, the trail was cold, and no one would listen to his theory of foul play. Even then, Benny Lewis had established a reputation of being a leader in the wine-growing community and a philanthropist. The police had even located a witness who'd seen a woman matching his aunt's description jump off this very pier.

What Jack knew for sure was that his aunt would never have taken her own life. The fact that the Lewis family had insisted on holding a memorial service for their late chef had infuriated him. Hotheaded and grief-stricken, he'd driven to the Lewis estate that day and accused Benny of having his aunt killed. From that moment, he'd been a persona non grata at the Lewis Winery, and a recent article he'd written, part of a series called "Crime Families in the Twenty-first Century," had rekindled the old animosity.

The cry of a gull overhead brought him back to the present. Shading his eyes, he watched the bird circle and then light on a second-story railing. For years, he'd nurtured a hope that his aunt might be alive. To this day, he was sure that he'd caught a glimpse of her at his college graduation ceremony. His roommate Franco had told him that it was just some kind of wish projection, but Jack hadn't been entirely convinced. Then there'd been the anonymous fan letters that he'd received during the eight years he'd spent abroad, covering stories and writing the articles that would become his first book. At times, he could have sworn he heard his aunt's voice and phrasing in them. But none of them had been signed, and the postmarks had all been from different places.

Turning, Jack glanced down at the dark water as it

pushed against the pilings. It had been twelve years, and it all came back to the same question. If his aunt was alive, why hadn't she ever contacted him in person? One thing he was sure of—Benny Lewis held the key to answering his questions.

With Corie at his side and the threat of scandal if the story of an illegitimate daughter wasn't handled "properly" in the press, Benny Lewis would have to finally grant him an interview. Then he could complete his work on crime families and send it off. His publisher was already pressuring him to think about a series of articles on the Middle East, so the clock was ticking.

Jack pushed himself away from the railing and began to pace. Why in hell wasn't he celebrating the fact that he'd convinced Corie Benjamin to fly out here?

"You got a problem, you face it head-on." That's what his aunt's advice would have been. Well, his problem was Corie Benjamin. He'd never before been so curious about a woman. The more he got to know her, the more puzzling she became.

There was her voice for one thing. At times, there was a shyness in it that went hand in hand with the image he'd formed of her in his mind—mousy hair tied into a bun, a baggy sweater worn with a shapeless dress and sensible shoes.

Frowning, Jack gazed out across the water. But at other times there was a hint of steel beneath the soft tone. He'd heard it loud and clear when she'd demanded that makeover.

"What in hell do I know about arranging for a woman to get a makeover?" He couldn't imagine any other woman in his acquaintance admitting that they even wanted one.

"She's different, Aunt Mel."

And that was part of the problem. Corie Benjamin *was*

different. And he hadn't been completely honest with her. If he had, she probably would have stayed in Fairview. So maybe that was why he felt so...protective of her.

"But I was right to persuade her to come out here." He had to believe that. Lifting his hands from the railing, he rubbed them over his face. What was the matter with him? Corie Benjamin was going to be perfectly safe. Benny Lewis certainly wasn't going to jeopardize his reputation as one of San Francisco's leading philanthropists just because his long-lost daughter showed up, not when the mayor was going to honor him for the new wing that was being dedicated at the San Francisco Memorial Hospital this coming Friday.

"There isn't a safer time for her to make her appearance in his life." Even though he'd been over and over it in his mind, it helped him to say it out loud. "And everything should run like clockwork."

Jack lifted a hand and rubbed at the back of his neck to ease a prickling sensation. He felt as if someone was watching him. As his heart began to race, he whirled and scanned the pier.

Empty—except for a man tapping a white cane along the wooden planks on the lower level. A blind man taking a morning stroll with his dog. So much for the strange feeling he'd had that he was being watched. Jack frowned again. He was going to have to get a grip on his nerves. A good reporter always kept a cool head.

He pushed himself away from the pier and started a slow jog back to his car.

2

JACK PULLED INTO HIS SLOT in the underground garage of his apartment building and opened the door. Before he could close it, Franco Rossi, his old college roommate and current landlord, hurried toward him.

"Well, do you think she got on the plane?"

During his globe-trotting years, Jack had met his share of colorful and eccentric characters, but Franco still remained at the top of the list. For the past eight years Franco had lived in New York City, subsidizing his acting career with a job as a doorman at a posh Central Park West apartment building, and he'd acquired an...unusual wardrobe.

"She told me she was coming, and I have a feeling that once Corie Benjamin makes up her mind, she sticks to it."

"Wonderful!" Franco rubbed his hands together. "Wonderful!" This morning he was wearing a bright red kimono, a souvenir from his performance in an off-Broadway production of *Tea House of the August Moon.* Beneath the spiked hair and the orange-rimmed sunglasses, who would suspect that there lurked a man who was a black belt in karate? And Jack was pretty sure no one would guess that Franco owned the apartment building he lived in. The lovely old Painted Lady had been his sole award in a palimony suit against his former longtime lover.

Franco whipped a notebook out of his pocket. "What

else do you know about her? I've decided she's the perfect heroine for my screenplay."

Jack urged Franco back into the building. "You say that about every woman you meet. Your place or mine?"

"Yours," Franco said, glancing at his watch. "My Monday-Tuesday tenant hasn't moved out yet. Besides, you have better coffee, and I just French-pressed a pot of your Arabica."

"Make yourself at home," Jack said dryly as Franco used his passkey to let them in. Until he sold his screenplay, Franco had decided to live as frugally as possible. Therefore, he was presently renting out his second-floor apartment on a per diem basis to two women who lived there on different days of the week while Franco had moved into the old maid's quarters in the basement.

Franco poured two cups of coffee and settled himself on the couch that swept around two walls of the sunny living room while Jack filled him in on what he knew about Corie Benjamin.

"So, the opening scene is eleven-fifteen at the airport. I can see it now. Sun pouring down through all that glass as our heroine walks wide-eyed through the gate into a brave new world." Grabbing the notebook that was never far from reach, Franco began to jot down notes.

"This isn't a movie," Jack said.

"It will be. Corie Benjamin's perfect—a shy little country mouse coming to the big city. My agent will be very excited about it."

"I thought he was interested in the other two plots you're hatching," Jack said.

"Those too." Franco waved his hand, then continued to scribble notes.

Jack moved to the window. Across the street, the construction workers were taking their places on the scaffolding that decorated two houses. In a matter of moments, a cacophony of ear-numbing noises would begin.

Turning back to Franco, he said, "I told her that she could use your apartment for the entire week and perhaps more, if she decides to extend her stay."

"No problemo. I spoke with the two women who use the apartment now on different days, and I'm sure she can work something out with them."

"There's just one more thing." Jack ran a hand through his hair. "She wants a makeover—the kind they're always doing on TV talk shows. Do you know what she's talking about?"

Franco glanced up. "A makeover! That will be perfect. It's just what I needed—a Pygmalion theme. Eliza Doolittle meets Vito Corleone! That is sooo high concept! My agent will definitely be able to sell it!"

Jack crossed to the couch and sat down. Sometimes his friend needed a firm hand. Taking Franco's notebook and pen, he then set them on the table. "Forget about the screenplay for a minute. Can you handle the makeover for me?"

Franco's brows shot up. "Is rain wet? Do flowers bloom in the spring? When my mother first read me *Cinderella*, I didn't want to be the prince. I wanted to be the fairy godmother. I've always wondered why I wasn't born with a magic wand in my hand."

Jack's eyes narrowed. "You're going to do it yourself?"

"Heavens no. I'll be her advisor, but I'll probably enlist the help of Lorenzo. He's currently doing my hair."

Jack frowned. "I don't think she is envisioning spikes."

"Relax. Lorenzo is one of the top hair designers in San Francisco. He does all the movie stars when they visit. Our little Corie will be in good hands."

Jack's frown deepened. "That's just it. She's not our little Corie."

Franco studied Jack for a moment. "For someone who spent the past two weeks convincing our little Cor—librarian to board that plane tomorrow, you don't look very happy."

Shoving his hands in his pockets, Jack began to pace. "If there was some other way that I could gain access to the Lewis family, I wouldn't have involved her."

"You worry too much."

"Maybe I haven't worried enough. I still don't know who sent me the anonymous e-mail, telling me about her and where to locate her."

"Why don't you ask your friend at Cop Central to help you out?"

Jack had thought about that. His friendship with Captain D. C. Parker went back to their high school days. "I couldn't ask D.C. to do anything illegal. He's on the political fast track in the department."

Franco shrugged. "Who says he'd have to get involved? All you need is a name—someone who's had a few brushes with the law...."

Jack paused in his pacing to study his friend. "You know, with a devious mind like yours, you'd make a good journalist."

Franco threw up his hands. "Not on your life! I'll stick to my screenplay, thank you. And I think you really ought to relax about this. Even if all your suspicions about Benny Lewis turn out to be true, he's worked too hard to build his reputation as a pillar of the community and a philanthropist to risk even the barest hint of scandal at this point. Our little Corie is going to be perfectly safe."

"You're right. I know you're right." *But...* Jack barely kept himself from saying the word out loud.

Franco leaned back against the cushions on the couch. "You know, I've never seen you this concerned about a woman before."

Jack considered that for a moment. He made a point of never becoming too involved with a woman. He'd always told himself that it was because he was never in one place for long, and he had no business taking on the responsibility. But he didn't have to go to a shrink to figure out that he didn't trust long-term relationships. He'd lost his parents when he was five and his aunt when he was eighteen. Nothing lasted. Therefore, it was just...easier not to get involved. And he didn't intend to get involved with Corie Benjamin. It was just that... "I've never met anyone like her before. She's different. And she wouldn't be coming out here to meet her father if I hadn't called her."

"Is she pretty?" Franco asked.

"How would I know? I've never seen her." But he wanted to. For the first time, it occurred to him that he was looking forward to meeting Corie for reasons that had nothing to do with his pursuit of the truth surrounding his aunt's disappearance. Suddenly, he frowned.

"Well, well, well. I never thought I'd see the day that a woman would tie you up in knots," Franco said.

"Don't be ridiculous. Corie Benjamin is not my type."

"Anything you say."

"I'm just feeling a little guilty because I never told her about Benny's early connections to the mob."

Franco's eyes widened. "That's a biggie."

"I kept telling myself that I'd do it as soon as she got out here. And now I feel responsible for her. If something should happen..."

"What could happen? You have labored under the suspicion that Benjamin Lewis had something to do with your aunt's disappearance far too long. The man's a pillar of the community, for heaven's sake. Sure, he supposedly had past mob connections, but not since he moved his family out here almost thirty years ago." Franco rose from the couch. "But just in case our little librarian is in any danger, I have the perfect backup plan. I thought I would store it here while my apartment is in use." Rising, he strode to the hall closet and drew out a hanger. "This," he gave the hanger a little shake and for a moment the black skirt hanging from it seemed to catch the light, "will protect her."

Jack shifted his gaze from the skirt to Franco. "That's a skirt."

"Indeed, it is—but it's a very special skirt. The fiber was woven from the lunua plant that grows only on this one island, and whoever wears the skirt has the power to draw men like a magnet. I'm trying to get in touch with the original owner, Torrie Lassiter. She lives here in San Francisco and I'm trying to track her down for an interview. Supposedly, she started everything by tossing the skirt instead of her bouquet at her wedding. Since then, this little skirt's become an urban legend."

"You're kidding, right?" Jack asked.

Franco raised his right hand, a solemn expression on his face. "I would never joke about this skirt. I've seen it in action. Since I've moved out here to San Francisco, I've given some thought to wearing it myself. Getting back into the dating scene is tough. It's a real wasteland out there." Franco shifted his gaze to the skirt. "Still... I'm not sure I'm ready. The skirt comes with a little catch."

"Most things do." Jack studied the skirt. It looked ordinary enough—simple, black, basic.

"Whoever wears this skirt will draw her true love to her," Franco said.

Jack studied his friend. He'd known Franco long enough

to know when he was joking. But he was serious. And he was sober. "Just how is a man-magnet skirt supposed to protect Corie Benjamin? She isn't coming out here looking for a man."

Franco held up a hand. "On the contrary. She *is* looking for one—her father. And the interesting thing about this skirt is that it has different effects on different men. It's been known to get some of the women who've worn it out of very tough scrapes—including ones involving guns and knives."

Moving forward, Franco spread the skirt out on one of the couch cushions. "I was going to talk Corie into wearing it anyway. Now I'll just fit it into the makeover. The skirt is the hook I'm using in my screenplay."

"Franco, I don't know…"

"What can it hurt?"

Reaching out, Jack fingered the material. For a moment, he was almost sure he caught a scent that reminded him of the kind of exotic flowers that would only grow on a tropical island. That was almost as ridiculous as the feeling of being watched that he'd gotten on the pier earlier.

Outside on the street, there was a loud sound like a gunshot. Dropping the skirt, Jack whirled back to the window in time to see a large black car give one lurch, then, tires squealing, race toward the corner.

Franco patted him on the shoulder. "That car was just backfiring. You should take something to calm your nerves."

But it wasn't the car or the backfiring that bothered Jack. It was the man he'd caught a glimpse of in the front seat of the car. A man wearing a hat and sunglasses with a dog on his lap. For a second, he was almost sure that it was the blind man he'd seen walking his dog at Fisherman's Wharf.

CORIE STEPPED OUT of the jet way and blinked at the bright sunlight streaming through the windows that ran along both walls of the airport. Well, she was here. Too late for regrets, she told herself as she pressed a hand against the mix of nerves and excitement bubbling away in her stomach.

Tightening her grip on her duffel bag, she glanced at the overhead signs and followed the arrows toward baggage pickup. Jack Kincaid would be there, and her San Francisco adventure would begin. She was determined to make the seven days count.

Eagerly she studied people around her, noting the tiny Chinese woman in the slim black pants and sandals, the Indian woman in a colorful sarong, a luxuriously built redhead in pencil-thin heels and a blue silk business suit that Corie bet cost more than she made at the library in a month. Only by force of sheer willpower did she keep herself from glancing down at her shapeless navy dress and serviceable shoes. In Fairview, she fit right in. In San Francisco she was a walking, breathing 9-1-1 fashion emergency.

Straightening her shoulders, she stepped onto the escalator that promised to take her to baggage claim. She was going to change her image as soon as she could, but for now, she had to focus on meeting Jack Kincaid and his friend with the unusual wardrobe. As she scanned the heads popping into view, she spotted the man who had to be Jack's friend.

Skimming her gaze over the lime-green walking shorts, orange polka-dot T-shirt and orange-rimmed sunglasses, Corie couldn't prevent a smile. The whole outfit seemed to work somehow. Then she shifted her attention to Jack Kincaid who was taller than his companion and dressed more conservatively in jeans and a tan linen sport coat. The two men made a very odd couple indeed. The shorter man placed a hand on Jack's arm, and Jack leaned closer to listen.

For the first time, it struck her that they might be just that—a couple. Jack *had* said he was bringing a "friend" to the airport, and this *was* San Francisco, after all. As she watched, Jack grinned at something his companion was saying. Then the dimple that she hadn't been able to keep from touching on his book jacket was there, too, appearing and disappearing as his grin deepened or faded. What would it feel like to press her finger into that dimple?

The thought had her stopping dead in her tracks.

It wasn't wise to be thinking about touching Jack Kincaid. Especially since it appeared that he already had someone to touch his dimple. Besides, hadn't she decided that Jack was just the kind of man her mother had warned her about? "He will lie to you, and you will believe him."

Well, she wouldn't believe him—not entirely. In the two days since she'd made her decision to use the plane ticket Jack had sent her, Corie had clarified her goals, and she had a notebook full of doodles to prove it. The library had given her one week off, and she was determined to make the most of it. Not only was she going to meet the man who might be her father and find out why her mother had run away to hide, but she was also going to live it up while she was in San Francisco. She was going to do things she might never have the opportunity to ever do in Fairview— not with Muriel Ponsonby and the quilting circle hovering over her. One thing she was sure of. When she returned, no one was ever going to even think of her in the same sentence as Harold Mitzenfeld again.

Moving forward, she caught what the two men were saying.

"You've got to tell her," the man with the green shorts was saying.

"I'm going to just as soon as I find the right time—after she settles in a bit," Jack replied.

Corie saw the other man's brows rise above the orange-framed sunglasses. "There's a *right* time to find out your family has a lurid past?"

Corie stepped forward. "Why don't you tell me right now?"

For a moment, the two men stared at her, and Corie had the sensation that she was being studied as thoroughly as a biologist might study a smear on a slide. No one had ever looked at her quite this closely back in Ohio. It made her wonder it she'd put her dress on inside out.

And then she made the mistake of looking into Jack's eyes directly. They were steel-gray, cool and very intent. Where in the world had she gotten the idea that he was charming? Without the dimple and the smile to distract her, she could see that this was an intense and driven man who watched and measured everyone. He reminded her a little of a Brontë hero—Rochester right after he'd nearly run Jane Eyre down with his horse.

Jack's friend was the first to recover. Holding out his hand, he said, "Franco Rossi, at your service. I'm Jack's landlord and yours, too. Welcome to San Francisco."

Pulling her gaze away from Jack's took some surprising effort, but Corie managed it, then beamed a smile at Franco. "Thank you, Mr. Rossi."

"Franco, please. We're going to be neighbors."

The moment Franco released her hand, Corie extended it to Jack. "What is it that you should have told—" The minute his hand clasped hers, her heart felt as if it had turned right over in her chest. Perhaps it was because she was drowning in those eyes. The longer she stared into them, the more they reminded her of fog hanging thick and dark over the cornfields in Ohio. It wasn't until he released her hand that she felt the weakness in her knees.

"Are you all right?"

It took her a moment to realize that Franco had asked the question, and another minute to grab on to a thought. Those Brontë heroes might have been short in the charm department, but she was sure her mother would have included them in her first commandment.

Gathering her scattered wits, Corie managed to drag her gaze away from Jack's and smile at Franco. "It must be jet lag. I felt a little dizzy there for a minute. But I never faint."

"Good to know," Jack murmured.

She risked a quick look at him and was pleased to note that this time her heart stayed right where it belonged. "What was it that you were going to tell me, Mr. Kincaid?"

"Jack, please." He smiled at her. "It's just some of the evidence that I told you about. We can talk about it over lunch." He glanced at the nearby beltway that had begun to move. "If you'll just point out your luggage, we'll be on our way."

Very smooth, Corie thought but she knew it was a lie. She was almost sure that Franco had been pressing him to tell her about Benny Lewis's past.

"This is my luggage," she said, indicating the duffel she was carrying.

Franco took it from her. "Then we're off to lunch and after that to Lorenzo's. He does my hair." He gave her a little shove into the revolving doors.

When Jack joined her on the street, he said, "Franco says Lorenzo is the top choice of the Hollywood starlets when they come to town. And I told him that if you end up with spiked hair, I'll have to kill him."

She couldn't prevent the laugh. And this time when she

met his eyes, it was her stomach that seemed to lurch and then tighten. She threw all her effort into dragging her gaze away from his, and that was the only reason that she saw the man with the gun.

Later, she would recall the other details—that the man holding it was standing by the open door of a car, that he wore a hat and dark glasses and a dog sat patiently next to the white cane he was holding in his left hand. But, at the moment, all that fully registered in her mind was the gun.

A woman screamed. "He's got a gun!"

"A gun!"

There was another scream and people at the curb began to scatter. As they cleared, Corie had enough time to see the man raise his hand and point the gun into the air. Then someone pushed her into Jack. It was like colliding with a brick wall.

"Get down," she said.

The sound of the shot split the air, drowning out her words, but Jack was already shoving her to the ground.

3

"LORENZO WILL SQUEEZE YOU IN AT TWO," Franco announced, closing his cell phone and signaling a waitress. "When Cameron Diaz was late for an appointment, he made her wait three days before he rescheduled." Pausing, he leaned closer to Corie. "Thank heavens I knew him when he was Billy Lawrence from Trenton."

Jack leaned back in his chair as a waitress slapped down three menus.

"Three Irish coffees," Franco ordered before anyone could speak. Then he turned to Corie. "It's the house specialty. They claim credit for originating the drink here in the U.S., and a shot of strong Irish whiskey will do us all good after that unfortunate incident at the airport."

Unfortunate incident? Jack studied the two people at the table and stifled the urge to pinch himself. Franco punched more numbers into his cell phone, and Corie stared out the window of the café, looking for all the world like Eliza Doolittle getting her first glimpse of Henry Higgins's world. Was he the only one who was worried about the "blind" gunman who had shot at them at the airport?

Both Franco and Corie had gotten a look at the shooter. Franco had noticed that the shooter had been wearing a fedora and a tan trench coat. Corie had described the gunman as an older man wearing sunglasses with a white cane and she'd caught just a glimpse of a small, fluffy dog.

The moment she'd spoken the words *white cane* and *dog*

to the policeman, the hairs on the back of his neck had sprung to attention. Could it have been the same man he'd seen earlier at Pier 39—and later in the car that had backfired in front of his apartment building? That was the question that had been plaguing him as Franco had bundled them into his SUV and driven them to Fisherman's Wharf. Jack wished that he'd gotten a look at the shooter, but he'd been so focused on getting Corie out of the line of fire, he hadn't been any help at all. What were the chances of seeing two older men with sunglasses, white canes and dogs in one morning? Ordinarily, Jack didn't believe in coincidences, but in this case the incident was so...bizarre.

And it had all happened so fast. Even now, his memory of the shooting came in flashes—the deafening sound of the shot, the fear he'd felt when Corie crashed into him, screams and then the screech of tires. He hadn't seen the gunman at all.

Was he crazy to think that the "blind" man had been shooting at Corie? She'd told the police that the man had fired straight into the air, and several other witnesses had corroborated her account. However, his instincts—the ones that seemed to be operating overtime when it came to Corie—told him not to exclude the possibility that Corie might be in danger. But he didn't have one shred of evidence, and the police were going with the theory that the gunman was a crackpot who'd fired blindly over the heads of the crowd. That was the slant that Jack had taken when he'd phoned the story into the *Chronicle.* The afternoon headline would read Blind Gunman Causes Havoc At Airport.

Franco flipped his cell phone closed with a flourish. "Mission accomplished. Marlo, my friend at Macy's, is rescheduling your fashion consultation for five. That will put a little pressure on Lorenzo, but he's a genius." He beamed a smile at Corie. "By tonight, you won't recognize yourself. We'll go out on the town to celebrate. There's a great new place in the neighborhood, Club Nuevo. Lots of singles hang out there."

"Maybe Corie would like to rest," Jack said.

"Nonsense." Corie and Franco spoke in unison and then grinned at each other.

Jack found that the exchange made him feel like an outsider. More than that, it made him feel...jealous?

That was ridiculous. But perhaps not as ridiculous as the fact that he was attracted to Corie Benjamin. The moment that he'd taken her hand and looked into her eyes, he'd felt the pull—basic, elemental. And he'd wondered what it might be like between them. Hell, he was wondering what it might be like to make love to her right now. And that was more than ridiculous. It was impossible. He was responsible for her now that he'd gotten her to come to San Francisco. And she might be in danger. He was definitely not going to act on any attraction he felt for Corie Benjamin.

"Look, Corie." Franco pointed to the bar. "You don't want to miss the way they make the Irish coffees here."

Corie turned in the direction that Franco was pointing. The bartender had a row of glass cups in front of him. With one hand he added whiskey to each and with the other a dollop of whipped cream. She might have enjoyed watching the ritual more if she hadn't been so aware of Jack sitting next to her. Every time he looked at her, prickles of heat raced along her skin and triggered a strange and rather pleasant tightening in her stomach. The sensations were even stronger now than when she'd first looked into his eyes at the airport. She'd never experienced anything like this before.

Jet lag. That had to be it. But she couldn't help remembering what it had felt like to lie beneath him for those few moments on the sidewalk at the airport. The press of his body against hers, as impersonal as it had been, had set her mind wondering and her body wanting.

Definitely jet lag. He'd never given her any indication that he was attracted to her. As a ripple of applause began at the bar, she stole a quick look at Jack. Up close, he was much more attractive than he'd been on his book cover. Though it shocked her, she found that she couldn't look at that longish dark hair without wanting to run her hands through it. And she had to clasp her hands tightly in front of her to control the urge to touch that lean, tanned face.

Her gaze dropped to his mouth. His lips were thin, masculine, and set in a grim line. Something tightened inside of her, and she could almost feel what it might be like to have those lips pressed against hers. They would be hard, demanding...

Wrenching her gaze away, Corie stared out the window until her heart slid back out of her throat and stopped beating like a bass drum. If she'd been alone, she would have taken out her notebook and tried to doodle her way to some understanding of what she was feeling. Then again, if she were alone, she wouldn't be feeling this way, and she was beginning to like it. The man she'd had an affair with in college hadn't even once made her feel the way she did when she just looked at Jack Kincaid. She risked another quick glance, but Jack was looking at Franco. Her heart sank. Could Jack be having the same thoughts about Franco that she was having about Jack? When a strange bitter-tasting flavor filled her mouth, Corie blinked.

Could it be jealousy she was feeling? Ridiculous. There wasn't a chance in the world that Jack Kincaid could be attracted to her. Besides, hadn't she read somewhere that all the best men were gay? So it was hopeless anyway.

"Enjoy," the woman said as she delivered their coffees and hurried on to the next table.

"To Corie's San Francisco adventure," Franco said, raising his glass.

Jack didn't lift his. "We have to talk."

Corie and Franco both turned to him.

"Am I the only one who's at all worried about the shooting incident at the airport?"

Franco's eyes narrowed. "What are you saying?"

"I don't like the timing." Pausing, Jack rubbed the back of his neck. "I've been thinking it over, and it's possible that the shooter was aiming at Corie."

Franco whipped out his notebook. "A blind hit man. What a plot point!"

Corie set down her coffee. "He fired the bullet into the air. I saw him and so did several other witnesses. The police concluded he was just some crazy person."

Jack gave Franco an annoyed look before returning his gaze to Corie's. "I have a feeling—the same one I get whenever something I'm working on is about to go bad. And I just want to cover all the possibilities so that we can take precautions. It's possible that someone in the Lewis family might not be too thrilled that you're here."

Corie's expression became thoughtful as she considered it for a moment. "True. But how did the Lewis family know I was arriving today?"

"The person who e-mailed me your whereabouts could also be feeding the Lewises the same information," Jack said.

"Okay. But if they're so worried, why did they send a blind hit man to shoot at me?"

"Good point," Franco said and made a note.

"Okay," Jack raised both hands, palms out. "You've got logic on your side there. But what if the white cane and the dark glasses were a disguise? Maybe he could see perfectly well, and he just dressed that way to get close to you or to make sure that he couldn't be identified."

"He's got a point," Franco remarked as he scribbled on the page.

"Let me get this straight. He could see perfectly?" Corie asked with a smile. "So perfectly that he aimed his bullet into the air and completely missed me."

"Now, she's got a point. I feel like I'm at a tennis match." Franco's pen never stopped moving on the page.

A tennis match where he wasn't scoring many points off his opponent, Jack thought. She had a sharp mind, and at any other time he would have enjoyed matching wits with her. "Look. It's just possible that I might have seen the shooter this morning when I was running at Pier 39. I saw a blind man there, too, and he was walking his dog. I can't be sure it was the same man, but later I thought I saw him again in a car that backfired in front of our apartment building. He could have followed me there and then out to the airport." He ran a hand through his hair. "And there's something else I haven't told you about Benny Lewis."

Corie nodded. "You're referring to the fact that Benny Lewis used to have mob connections."

Jack stared at her. "You *know* about that?"

Franco flicked a glance at Jack. "She's not the naive little librarian we thought she was."

Corie's brows shot up as she shifted her gaze from one man to the other. "It would be a rare librarian indeed who could still be *naive* with the information highway at her fingertips. I researched everything about the man who might be my father. One of the most informative articles I found was written by one Jack Kincaid for the *San Francisco Chronicle*. It traced Benny Lewis's family back to one of the first organized crime families in this country." She met Jack's eyes steadily. "And it revealed that you are not welcome on the Lewis estate. I figure that's one of the reasons you invited me out here. I'm your leverage to get an interview, or whatever it is you're after."

"Busted," Franco murmured.

Jack felt the heat rising in his neck. "I was going to tell you. I just didn't want to do it over the phone."

"In your article, you also said that the Lewis Winery and the Crystal Water Spa are legitimate businesses, and that Benny Lewis cut all ties to his organized crime confederates over thirty years ago when he moved out here. Do you have any reason to believe otherwise?"

"Just a feeling."

"It's a feeling that Jack's been nursing for twelve years or so—ever since I've known him," Franco put in. "He's got nothing to substantiate it."

Corie frowned thoughtfully. "But if you could connect the gunman at the airport to Benny, then you'd have something more than a feeling, right?"

"The plot thickens," Franco said.

Jack glared at him. "This isn't a screenplay."

Corie took a sip of her Irish coffee, then looked at him. "We should get going right away."

"You want to go back to Fairview." Jack didn't blame her.

"Of course not," Corie said taking another sip of her coffee.

Jack stared at her. He couldn't quite keep up with her. She wasn't angry that he hadn't mentioned the Lewis family's early organized crime connections, nor did she seem to be frightened. "Let me get this straight. You've known all along that Benny Lewis had mob connections in his past, and now you know that I think he still might. Aren't you worried at all?"

"Not really. But I didn't come out here with blinders on. If Benny Lewis is my father, then twenty-six years ago something happened to make my mother run away and live the life of a recluse. I took two weeks to decide whether or not I wanted to come out here and open up that can of worms. And I do. So let's get started. If there is a connection between that blind gunman at the airport and the Lewis family, then it might have something to do with why my mother hid away all these years. What's your plan?"

"Plan?"

"Plot point number two. Hero and heroine join forces to solve the crime," Franco said as he scribbled. "Shades of *The Thin Man*."

Corie turned to Franco. "I just love those movies. Nick and Nora Charles were the perfect partners." She turned back to Jack. "When can we get started?"

Jack frowned. "No. Absolutely not. I don't work with a partner. I work alone."

"But you invited me out here, and you need me to gain access to Benny."

In the short beat of silence that followed, Franco cleared his throat. "She's got you there."

Then Corie and Franco merely waited, watching him expectantly. The shy little librarian had a mind like a steel trap and a dogged determination that surprised him and drew his admiration at the same time. Until he figured out how to handle her, his best strategy was to distract her.

"My plan is simple. I'm going to take you to a party Friday night—a reception following the dedication of the new children's wing at San Francisco Memorial Hospital. It's being held at the Monahan House, one of San Francisco's newest and most exclusive hotels. A close friend of mine, Jake Monahan, owns the hotel, and so he's going to see that we get into the reception."

"Why can't I meet Benny sooner?" Corie asked.

"He's out of the country visiting a new winery that he purchased in southern Italy. He'll be flying back on Thursday evening specifically for the party on Friday. He and the whole family will be there. It's a public affair. I figure it's your best scenario for meeting him."

"And you're just going to walk up to Benny and introduce me as his long-lost illegitimate daughter?"

"No. I'll introduce you as Corie Benjamin." He drew a photo out of his pocket and placed it in front of her. "Since you look almost exactly like your mother, I'm assuming that he'll agree to speak with you in a more private arena."

Corie stared down at the old picture. The first thing that struck her was that the woman sitting in the restaurant booth next to the darkly handsome man could have been her twin sister. Over the years, she had grown used to comments that she and her mother looked alike, but now she was facing concrete evidence of it.

"You're sure this man is Benny Lewis?" she asked.

"Yes," Jack said. "I've got several other photos of him from that time period."

Corie felt the prick of tears at the back of her eyes. The man in the picture was so handsome, and the charm was so evident in his smile. Her mother looked so young, and so happy. She touched a finger to the woman's face and for the first time she let herself believe that the man in the picture might indeed be her father. A rush of feeling moved through her, tightening her throat and squeezing into a little band around her heart. She would be meeting him in a little more than thirty-six hours.

Raising her eyes to meet Jack's, she said, "I was hoping, but I didn't really believe it before."

He reached out and took her hand.

Linking her fingers with his, she met Jack's gaze steadily. "I do now. I really think he's my father. And I'm not going to let some crazy man at the airport scare me away."

"Here! Here!" Franco said as he raised his mug in another toast.

Corie took a sip of her coffee and then said, "But Friday is two days away. Shouldn't we be investigating something in the meantime? We could go out to the winery and look for a man with a dog wearing sunglasses and a fedora and carrying a white cane."

Jack bit back a grin. Not only was Corie smart and determined, but she wasn't going to be easily distracted. "If he was wearing a disguise, he won't be wearing it the next time we see him."

"Good point," Franco said. "You two are about even right now."

"And you have an appointment at Lorenzo's at two o'clock," Jack added.

Franco raised his glass again. "To the new Corie Benjamin."

Jack took a long swallow of his Irish coffee. While Corie was safely occupied at Lorenzo's, he was going to modify and expand his plan. First, he was going to have a heart to heart with D. C. Parker down at the homicide division. He needed to know exactly who was e-mailing him. Fast.

Mrs. H,

Just a little update on my research...

I have another great idea—and another great heroine for my screenplay. Renting out my apartment has not only been a financial boon, but it has also increased my creativity. Scenes are just flowing into my mind.

Corie Benjamin, my latest tenant, is a whole lot more than the shy little librarian I was expecting. I have a feeling she's more than my friend Jack was expecting, too! When they met for the first time at the airport, it was as if they were the only two people in the baggage claim area! I'm thinking *West Side Story*, the dance at the gym—when Tony and Maria meet for the first time and for a moment time stands still.

And it's my job to give the little librarian a make-over. We're at Lorenzo's salon as I'm writing this, and then we're off to see a personal shopper at Macy's. Picture the shopping scene from *Pretty Woman*.

And she hasn't even tried on the skirt yet! I can't wait to see what happens when Jack sees her in it! Picture *Sabrina* when the chauffeur's daughter comes back from Paris totally transformed! My agent is going to go ballistic!

Ta,

Franco

THE WAITING ROOM of Lorenzo's salon offered a view of the bay and the Golden Gate Bridge. Corie might have enjoyed it even more if it hadn't been for the tight knot of nerves in her stomach.

She'd never experienced anything like the salon, from the red-and-gold brocade drapes and Persian rugs to the exotic scents wafting into the room at regular intervals. But Corie had a hunch that the real cause of the nerves was the fact that Jack Kincaid had taken his leave of them and headed to the *Chronicle* office. She pressed a hand to her stomach. Silly to feel so alone just because a man she'd met only a few hours ago had left her.

At Franco's request, Nadia, a pencil-thin girl who had at least seven earrings in each ear, had brought her a glass of white wine. Noting that her knuckles had turned white from gripping the stem, Corie concentrated on relaxing her fingers. She had to get a grip.

At Jack's request, Rollo, the doorman at the salon, had agreed to watch out for her and, if the need arose, ward off any blind gunmen, until Jack could return. A huge barrel of a man with a shiny bald head, Rollo had stood blocking the doorway ever since Jack had left. But it wasn't the threat of blind gunmen with dogs that had her stomach doing flips.

"Drink up," Franco said, clinking his glass to hers. "There's no need to be nervous. Lorenzo had incredible talent even when I first knew him back in the Big Apple. He took a couple of acting classes with me at New York University. Lorenzo and I were theater majors. Jack was taking writing and journalism classes, so I'm not sure he would even remember Lorenzo."

"You've known Jack for a long time then?" Corie asked.

"Since our first year in college."

"Were you and Jack..." She hesitated. It really wasn't any of her business. "Were you involved even then?"

"Involved?"

Whatever else Franco might have said was cut off as a tall, golden god swept into the room. For a moment all Corie could think of was Ian Fleming's *Goldfinger*. The man—Lorenzo, she assumed—looked as if he'd been literally dipped in a rich shade of coppery gold—from the tone of his skin to the flow of hair that he wore swept back from his wide forehead. Even his eyes were a deep shade of amber.

"Lorenzo!" Franco rose and within seconds he all but

disappeared into the folds of the large man's flowing caftan.

"And you." Lorenzo released Franco and swept down on her, grasping her hand and drawing her to her feet in one smooth motion. Then, tipping her chin up, he studied her. "You must be the little librarian."

Corie would have nodded, but his grip on her chin was firm.

"Nadia?" He snapped the fingers of his free hand, and the pencil-thin woman whipped out a notebook. "The bones are good." He paused to trace a finger down Corie's cheek. "The skin is flawless. But the hair." He lifted a strand and shuddered, sending a rippling wave through his caftan. "It will have to go."

Corie felt the arrow of panic shoot right through her. She opened her mouth, but no sound came out.

"How much time do I have, Franco?"

"I've pushed back the appointment at Macy's until five."

"I have only three hours?" Lorenzo drew in a deep breath. Out of the corner of her eye, Corie saw Franco and Nadia both take a quick step back. She might have herself, but Lorenzo had never released her chin.

"Well! It's a good thing I'm a genius. Prep her, Nadia." Dropping his hand, Lorenzo whirled and sailed from the room.

"If you'll follow me, Ms. Benjamin?"

Corie raised a hand to her hair. She didn't think she could move.

Franco grabbed her arm and urged her toward the door that Lorenzo had disappeared through. "He likes you."

"He likes me?" Corie asked. "He wants to scalp me."

"No, no, no," Franco patted her arm as he pulled her

past a long row of curtained booths. "He's talking about a color and styling, and he's the best."

"Franco, I don't think—"

He pushed her into a chair. "And you shouldn't think. Just relax and put yourself in the hands of a master. Nadia, we need more wine." The moment the girl disappeared, he continued, "You have that party Friday night. You do want to look your best when you meet your family."

Corie faced herself in the mirror and barely kept herself from wincing. Even scalped, she had to look better than the way she looked now. The boring librarian look had to go. But even as Nadia reentered and pressed another glass of wine into her hand, her mother's words echoed in her ears.

Be careful what you wish for.

4

JACK PUSHED THROUGH the doors and strode into the large room that housed San Francisco's homicide detective division. Past the collection of desks in the bullpen area and down the corridor to his left, he found the door with D. C. Parker's name on it. He knocked once before he entered, then trained his best smile on the small but stout dragon who guarded the entrance to Captain Parker's lair.

"Ms. Abernathy." He whipped out the bunch of daffodils he held behind his back. "I saw these and thought of you."

Lydia Abernathy sniffed audibly, but she took the flowers. "Softening me up will get you nowhere, Mr. Kincaid. Captain Parker won't see you unless he wants to."

"I don't want to," growled a voice from the adjacent room. "Protect me, Ms. Abernathy. Throw the man out."

Lydia rolled her eyes, and Jack winked at her as he moved smoothly around her desk and through the half-open door. "He's a little grumpy because I won fifty bucks from him at poker last night," Jack told her. "It's a good thing for you he's better at police work than he is at cards."

"You were just lucky," D.C. complained.

"Yeah." Jack grinned at him as he turned a straight-backed chair around and straddled it. "I was."

"I hear you were lucky again at the airport," D.C. said.

"Yeah."

D.C.'s office was small and ruthlessly organized. File drawers were closed, and not even a stray pencil lay out of place on the gleaming mahogany desk. He'd known D.C. since their days in high school and he hadn't changed one bit. Jack thought briefly of his own office, cluttered with files and old notebooks filled with interview notes, and decided he hadn't changed much either.

"If you came to pump me for information about the blind shooter, everything I know is either in the papers or on CNN, thanks to you damn reporters."

Jack shook his head. "I don't think we've got everything. I'll bet what you lost at poker last night that you know the breed of the dog by now."

"Shit."

Jack grinned at him. "I'll take that as a yes."

D.C. sighed in disgust. "This is not for publication."

"Agreed."

"We just identified the breed from a sketch one of our artists made. It's a shih tzu, and we're trying to trace local owners through breeders. We'd like to keep it out of the press coverage for now."

"No problem. You got anything else?"

"Shih tzus are not bred as Seeing Eye dogs."

"So the cane and the glasses were likely a disguise." Leaning back in his chair, Jack studied his old friend. There was something else. He could tell it by the expression on D.C.'s face. "What else?"

"One witness swears that she saw a tall man, maybe in his late thirties, and he wasn't wearing a fedora or a trench coat. Nor did she see a dog. She says he pocketed a gun and ducked into a car right after the shot was fired."

"Two shooters?" He didn't like the sound of that at all.

"That's the million-dollar question, and the answer is up for grabs. Eyewitnesses are never reliable, and there's always the witness who'll embroider a story just for the extra attention. But I've got some calls into informants. Nobody likes guns anywhere near airports. If there *were* two shooters, the two-million-dollar question is who were they shooting at? You got any idea?''

"Maybe. But I need two favors."

"Yeah, like I didn't know that when you walked through that door."

"First, I'd like to know who owns that dog as soon as you get it."

D.C. studied his friend. "You know something, don't you?"

"Maybe."

D.C. pulled out a notebook. "Fill me in."

Jack did, beginning with the first e-mail message he'd gotten from his anonymous informant and ending with the shot at the airport and his gut feeling that the Lewis family was involved.

D.C. was frowning when Jack finished. "You're big on theory and short on evidence." He raised a hand to ward off Jack's comments. "First of all, there's nothing that links either gunman to the Lewis family."

"Yet," Jack said. "I'm hoping the dog will."

For a moment, D.C. said nothing. He was a man who made a point of not wasting words, and he'd said it all before, beginning when they were eighteen and D.C. had stood at Jack's side during the memorial service for his aunt. D.C. had never been as convinced as Jack that the Lewis family had had something to do with his aunt's disappearance.

In the silence that lengthened between them now, Jack heard the words in his mind as clearly as he had when D.C. had spoken them on the day of his aunt's memorial service. *You're too close to this, Jack. You aren't being objective.*

"Are you and this librarian involved?" D.C. finally asked.

It was the last question Jack expected his friend to ask. "No. I just met her when she stepped off that plane."

D.C. shot him a grin. "I've known you to work pretty fast before."

"We're not involved," Jack repeated.

"Too bad." D.C. tapped his fingers on the desk. "You know, I can't get her any official protection."

"She'll be staying at my apartment building for the next two days."

"Uh-huh."

"In another apartment," Jack said. "She's not my type."

D.C. held up two hands, palms out. "If you say so."

"How about some help with another problem? The only person I've told about Corie other than you is Franco and he's sworn to secrecy. But there's one other person who knows she lives in Fairview, and who could have accessed what flight she'd be on. He also could have given that information to someone in the Lewis family."

"Your anonymous informant," D.C. said.

"Have you got someone who's good at tracing e-mails?"

"Not on the city payroll." D.C. flipped through a Rolodex on his desk and then wrote on a piece of paper. "He's fifteen, and you didn't get his name from me."

"Fifteen?"

"He's got a real knack, and he's good enough to keep one step ahead of the law—so far."

Jack grinned as he took the slip of paper and rose.

"Keep me posted," D.C. said.

"Ditto," Jack said.

JACK SLUNG HIS COAT over the back of his office chair and glanced at his watch for the fifth time since he'd left D.C.'s office. He'd checked in with Franco twice since he'd left them at Lorenzo's. There wasn't a doubt in his mind that

Corie was safe. Rollo, the doorman, had promised to keep an eye on her.

He was overreacting. He seemed to be doing that a lot where Corie was concerned. Running a hand through his hair, he thought about that for a minute. No other woman had ever aroused his protective instincts the way she did. He'd always known what he wanted and what he didn't want from a relationship with a woman and responsibility had never been on his agenda.

Whoa. Where had that little word "relationship" come from? He was not about to have a relationship with Corie Benjamin. He might be attracted to her. All right. He *was* attracted to her. But he was not going to act on that attraction. He was going to introduce her to her father and get his interview with Benny. And for as long as she was in San Francisco, he would make sure that she was safe. Period.

Right now he had work to do. In fifteen minutes, D.C.'s hotshot computer expert was going to arrive. He clicked onto his e-mail, but there was nothing new from his anonymous tipster. After scrolling back to the last message, he clicked on Reply and typed,

What kind of game are you playing? Someone took a shot at Corie at the airport—an old man carrying a white cane with a ball-of-fluff dog.

The moment he clicked Send, he flipped open his cell phone and punched in Franco's number. When his friend answered, Jack said, "Is she all right?"

"She's fine—if you don't count the fact that she's wired up with enough strips of aluminum in her hair right now to attract transmissions from outer space."

Jack glanced at his watch. Exactly five minutes had gone

by since he'd glanced at it the last time. "Something's come up. I'm not sure I can be there in time to escort you to Macy's."

"No problem. I'll ask Rollo to come along. Lorenzo won't mind. It's part of Rollo's job to protect celebrity clients."

"Make sure he stays until I can get there."

"Roger," Franco said. "Over and out."

A knock sounded on his door and Jack glanced up to see a skinny kid with curly hair and wire-framed glasses standing just outside in the hall.

The kid cracked his knuckles, and Jack immediately recognized a nervous habit he'd had when he was fifteen.

"You Jack Kincaid?"

"Yeah."

"I'm Hawthorne James."

Jack moved forward with his hand extended. "My friend D. C. Parker speaks very highly of you."

Hawthorne blushed as he shook Jack's hand. "Parker's okay. Whatcha got for me?"

"I want to get a street address on someone who's e-mailing me. He doesn't sign his name."

The kid was already moving past Jack to study the computer screen. After a moment, he cracked his knuckles and sat down.

"You think you can do it?" Jack asked.

"Sure." He began tapping keys.

Jack glanced at his watch. "What time do your parents want you home?"

Hawthorne didn't glance up from the screen. "They're both out of town. I can work until the job's finished. It might take me a while."

"I can't stay with you, but there's staff here at night. I'll alert them that you'll be working in my office. What about food? Or something to drink?"

"Can I get a pizza delivered?"

"I'll arrange it with the man at the desk. It's on the *Chronicle.*"

Hawthorne leaned back in his chair and cracked his knuckles. "You got another message."

Jack moved to look at the screen.

Corie Benjamin is in danger. It was a mistake to bring her to San Francisco. If you care about her safety, send her back to Fairview.

CORIE STARED at herself in the mirror, not blinking for fear the image might disappear and the old Corie might come back. She was willing to do almost anything to see that didn't happen.

"Outfit number one should take you to the office and..." Pausing, Marlo, a tall woman with a deep, husky voice, slipped the pale yellow blazer off Corie's shoulders with the flourish of a magician whipping a rabbit out of a hat. "What's beneath will get you through the cocktail hour, dinner and dancing."

Franco clapped his hands together. "Marlo, you're a genius."

Corie couldn't argue with that. She could barely recognize herself. The thin silk camisole and slim black skirt hugged curves she hadn't known she had. As for the high-heeled sandals with the straps—well, she wasn't sure she could dance in them, but she was willing to try. Looking the way she did, she thought she just might be willing to try anything. The transformation had begun at Lorenzo's salon. Her hair, inches shorter and shades lighter, framed her face in a sunny cloud. She couldn't prevent herself from running a hand through it and watching it settle magically back in place.

Of course, she knew that changing herself on the outside was just the first step. She was going to have to change herself on the inside, too. She ran a hand down her hip where the skirt clung like a second skin and felt a surge of confidence, not unlike what she'd felt at six when she'd spread her arms and leapt off her roof. Meeting her own eyes in the mirror, she lifted her chin. She wasn't going to fail this time.

"Any reservations I might have had about the skirt are gone," Marlo said. "I'm going to insist that our buyer find some for us to carry here at the store."

"There's an up-and-coming designer in New York named Daryl who sold a reasonable facsimile of the design to Bloomingdale's," Franco said. "I can give you his card, but the skirt that Corie's wearing is one of a kind. I've traced the original owner, Torrie Lassiter, here to San Francisco. She's married to Jake Monahan, the man who owns that posh hotel everyone's raving about, Monahan House. I'm trying to arrange an interview, and I can always ask her if there's any chance of getting any more like this one if you like."

Corie let her gaze drop to the skirt. It was the one item of clothing that Macy's hadn't provided. The moment they'd arrived, Franco had pulled it out of his shoulder bag and insisted that Marlo build a wardrobe around it.

And she had. Corie's favorite outfit was the one she was wearing. It made her feel different—confident…and sexy. She read somewhere that clothes made the woman, and she was beginning to believe that it was true. She could actually become the woman she saw in the mirror.

Franco leaned over, snagging the hem of the skirt between his thumb and forefinger. "This fabric was woven from the special fibers of the lunua plant, and it has a special effect on the male of the species.''

Marlo's eyes narrowed. "Is that true or merely something you're making up for that screenplay of yours?''

"I kid you not. Smell it.''

Marlo and Corie both leaned down closer to the part of the skirt that Franco held between his fingers.

"I don't smell a thing," Marlo said.

"Me either," Corie said.

"Not surprising." Franco drew in a deep breath. "The skirt appeals only to men. The scent reminds *me* of some exotic flower that could only grow in a steamy jungle.''

Marlo sent Corie a skeptical look.

"Wait," Franco said. "There's more. This skirt has also been known to protect the woman wearing it from knives and bullets.''

"Right," Marlo said, catching Corie's eye in the mirror and winking.

"You're kidding, right?" Corie asked, turning in a slow circle and craning her neck so that she could study the skirt from all angles.

Marlo leaned closer. "Perhaps the secret scent paralyzes enemies.''

"Go ahead. Mock me." Franco drew out his notebook and waved it. "But I have documented cases.''

Turning, Corie studied herself in profile. Though it fit like a dream, the skirt itself certainly looked ordinary enough to her—simple, basic, black—and much shorter than anything she'd ever worn in Fairview. An image filled her mind of wearing the black halter top and skirt while she sat across a bridge table from Harold Mitzenfeld. She was about to laugh at the absurdity of the image when she saw something flash in the mirror—a brief image that disappeared before it could fully register. Glancing quickly at her two companions, she saw that they were still engaged in their conversation.

"...has a definite effect on men, depending on their age," Franco was saying.

Neither had noticed anything, Corie decided. Had she imagined it? Slowly, she turned back so that she was facing her image again. This time the flash was brighter, the image clearer, and it was lasting. Corie's eyes widened. What she was looking at was Jack Kincaid standing behind her, his hands at her waist. She swore she could feel the heat of each one of his fingers pressing against her skin. And she wasn't wearing the skirt. She wasn't wearing anything at all, and neither was he. Then just as suddenly as it had appeared, the image in the mirror vanished, and she was there alone again, fully dressed.

This was a first. Corie couldn't recall ever having pictured herself naked with a man before. Could a plain black skirt really have even half the special powers Franco claimed it did?

And *if* the skirt had some kind of power that attracted men, wouldn't San Francisco be the perfect place to try it out? The thought was so tempting, and so unlike any she'd ever had before, that for a moment Corie stared at herself in shock. But if she was serious about becoming the woman in the mirror, discovering if she could attract a man would be a logical first step.

Be careful what you wish for. The words became a little chant in her head as she continued to study herself in the mirror. Why shouldn't she try to attract a man? Better still, why shouldn't she have at least one wild and wonderful fling with a man in San Francisco? Was that so much to ask? She'd been careful not to let herself believe that she'd really find a family here in San Francisco. But a fling?

Looking the way she did, surely she could accomplish that in the week she'd allowed herself.

"Corie, darling..."

"What?" she asked, dragging her eyes from her image in the mirror.

"I'd like to give the skirt a little test run—a demo if you like," Franco said. "Are you up for it?"

"Sure," she said. Why not? At least once in her lifetime, a girl had a right to give in to temptation. "Where are we going?"

Franco shot her a surprised look. "Nowhere. I'm just going to invite Rollo to step in. You don't mind?"

"No. But you did say we could go to that club of yours later?"

"Your wish is my command." Franco pulled the curtain of the dressing room back. "Rollo, could you come in here a minute?"

"Problem?" Rollo asked as he stepped into the room.

"No," Franco explained. "We just wanted to ask your opinion on Corie's outfit."

"Sure, but I have to leave in about ten—" Rollo's voice trailed off the moment he shifted his gaze to Corie.

As the silence stretched, Corie studied the large man. He looked as though he'd been frozen into a statue.

Franco waved a hand in front of Rollo's face.

Rollo didn't respond.

"Rollo?" Corie said. "Are you all right?"

At the sound of her voice, Rollo blinked and met her eyes. Then he closed the distance between them, dropped down to one knee in front of her and took her hand in his.

For one giddy moment, Corie thought he might propose.

Rollo merely continued to stare at her, a solemn expression on his face. "You don't have to worry, little lady. As long as you're in San Francisco, you've got yourself a personal bodyguard—24-7."

"Shades of *Camelot*," Franco murmured.

Corie didn't know what to say. A quick look at Franco didn't help. He was too busy scribbling and muttering. And Marlo was staring, nearly as frozen as Rollo had been. Corie glanced back at the large man kneeling in front of her. If she was going to have a protector, he certainly looked highly qualified. He nearly filled the dressing room, and she pitied anyone who ran into him in a dark alley. She cleared her throat. "What about your job at Lorenzo's?"

"Don't you worry about that. I'll make other arrangements at the salon." Releasing her hand, Rollo then rose and backed out of the dressing room.

"Amazing," Franco said. "Who said that chivalry was dead?"

"You've made a believer out of me," Marlo said.

Still a little giddy, Corie turned to stare into the mirror. She'd never had a man drop to his knees at her feet before. Could it really have been the skirt that made Rollo act that way? She couldn't help but wonder what might happen when Franco took her to the new club he'd talked about.

She ran her hand over her hip again, and she saw Jack step into the room. A quick glance over her shoulder assured her that he was really there, fully clothed, standing just inside the dressing room door. When she returned her gaze to the mirror, she saw that he was staring at the skirt just as Rollo had. That was all she had time to register before his gaze moved up to lock on hers in the mirror.

His eyes were so hot. The color reminded her of the billowing smoke that must have shot up from Thornfield the night that Rochester's wife set it on fire. She could feel the heat even at a distance of five feet. That had to be why she felt a strange melting sensation in her stomach.

Jack Kincaid was the perfect man to have a fling with. Just thinking about it made her breath catch and her pulse race. It was really too bad that he was gay.

THE MOMENT that his eyes met Corie's in the mirror, Jack could have sworn that everything else in the room seemed to fade. Though she was standing several feet away, he knew in that instant what it would feel like to have every inch of her body pressed against his. Desire tightened into a hard, tight ball in his stomach. The pull he was feeling was so strong that if Franco and the woman hadn't been standing in the small dressing room, he would have been tempted to go to Corie, to get her out of that halter and skirt and touch every inch of her....

He also knew with a certainty that frightened him that if he ever gave in to the urge to do just that, he might not be able to walk away from Corie Benjamin. And it was getting harder and harder to remember that his number one rule with a woman was always to walk away.

"Well, what do you think?" Franco asked.

In some part of his mind, Jack knew that Franco was talking to him.

"You might at least say something about her hair," Franco prompted.

Hair. Jack struggled to gather his thoughts, and for the first time he noticed that Corie's hair was lighter, and her face was different, too. Her eyes looked darker, and her mouth was slicked with something that made him yearn for a taste.

"He's speechless." Franco pulled out his pen and began to scribble. "You see what I mean, Marlo?"

"What was that designer's name? Daryl?" Marlo asked.

With great effort, Jack tore his gaze away from Corie's. He'd come here for a reason. The e-mail. Turning to Franco, he said, "If you're done here, I'd like to get Corie back to the apartment." If he got out of this room, he might be able to think.

"No," Corie said.

He turned back to her the minute the word sunk in.

"We're going to Franco's club. Have you forgotten?"

"It's not a good idea," Jack said. "I got another e-mail, and my anonymous informant thinks you're in real danger."

Corie lifted her chin. "I'll be perfectly safe at the club. Rollo has offered his services as my personal bodyguard for as long as I'm in San Francisco."

Jack sent Franco an inquiring look. "Rollo?"

"That's right. He's smitten with her," Franco said. "He's making arrangements with Lorenzo."

Smitten? Jack glanced back at Corie and tried to clear his mind. It had started to cloud the moment he'd walked into the dressing room and seen her in that mirror. Her chin was lifted, her hands were fisted on her hips, and desire curled again in his stomach.

"You're not going to talk me out of going to the club," she said. "I've come all the way to San Francisco, I've had to endure purple goo on my hair and wet, slimy leaves on my body. I didn't go through that torture to go home and go to bed."

In another minute he was going to have to give in to the urge to grab her. He had to get out of the small, cramped space and away from her scent, which was wrapping around him like some exotic flower twined around vines in a rain forest.

"All right," he said. "We'll go to Franco's club."

"End of Act One," Franco said, closing his notebook with a snap. "Pack everything up, Marlo, and send it to the apartment ASAP. We're off to Club Nuevo."

5

SIGHTS, SOUNDS, SMELLS—Corie was certain she'd never been bombarded by so many of them at once before. Club Nuevo was crowded, noisy and literally vibrating with the beat of the music blasting through large speakers. The slick chrome-and-glass interior was visible only in brief flashes of light. Still, Corie could see plenty.

The small, square tables were meant to seat two, so the hostess had led them to a banquette that lined one of the walls. Franco had pulled up a chair for himself and then left to fetch drinks at the bar. Rollo had snagged himself a table a short distance away.

Corie wasn't at all sure that having three escorts was the best strategy for meeting new men in a singles club. And sitting next to Jack Kincaid wasn't helping either. The fact that he'd kept a hand pressed against the small of her back or on her arm had given even the hostess the impression that they were a couple.

Men and women lined up three deep at the bar, and Corie could just spot Franco, chatting with a woman who towered over him. She should have gone with him. What good did it do to come to a singles bar if one didn't mingle? Or if one was seated altogether too close to a man who was unavailable?

The real problem was that she wanted Jack Kincaid to be available. She was attracted to him in a way she'd never been attracted to a man before. Now, squeezed into the banquette with him, she could feel his heat all along one side of her body. He was close, and the temptation to touch him was driving her crazy. If she shifted just a little, she could bring her leg into contact with his. If she dropped her hand, she could run it along his thigh. She could imagine what that lean, hard muscle might feel like beneath her palm. If she did it just once, maybe...

Drawing in a deep breath, Corie clasped her hands together on the table in front of her and squeezed hard.

Jack Kincaid was not the man she should be thinking of touching. He was not a man she should be wanting to have a wild and wonderful fling with. He was taken, and she was in a place filled with men who weren't.

"What do you think?"

Think? Corie gripped her hands together even more tightly. How was she supposed to think when Jack had brought his mouth so close to her ear that her brain cells were melting? Gathering whatever stray thoughts she could muster, she turned and found he'd angled his head so that his ear was now on a level with her lips. All she had to do was lean a little closer and...

Never act on impulse.

She had to say something. Anything.

When she didn't, Jack raised his head, angling it so that he could meet her eyes. "Are you all right?"

"Yes." Corie felt the vibration of sound in her throat, but a blast of drums prevented her from hearing the word. Jack must have read her lips, because she saw the concern fade from his eyes. Dropping her gaze to his lips was a mistake. A big one. The urge she'd had to press her mouth against his ear was nothing compared to the desire she had now to kiss him. His lips were barely an inch away. Just thinking about how they might feel pressed against hers made her skin feel icy and then hot. There was a drumbeat in her head that she thought was the sound of her own heart, and she could feel the ache she'd felt before twist into longing.

She was melting and leaning toward him when he straightened and began to scan the room. Corie made herself take a breath, and felt the air burn in her lungs. She saw Jack's gaze focus on the bar—looking for Franco? Of course, he was. Pressing a hand against the sudden sinking sensation in her stomach, she drew in another breath.

Thank heavens he'd moved when he had or she would have made a fool of herself. Clearly, her awareness of him and the response he triggered in her were one-sided. Inching a little away from him, she turned her attention back to the club scene.

This was her first night in San Francisco and she was looking for a man who was available. Narrowing her gaze, she focused on the three men besides Rollo who were seated close by. Should she walk over to one of them?

Maybe Jack would have some advice. Turning, she pitched her voice so that he could hear without leaning down again. "Do you come here often?"

He glanced at her. "No. I've never been here before."

She studied him for a minute. Hadn't Franco said that this was one of his favorite clubs? Did Franco come here alone? Maybe he and Jack had one of those so-called open relationships. She turned to search the crowd at the bar for Franco, but just then her gaze locked with a man two tables away. In the intermittent flashes of light, she had trouble making out his features. All she could see for sure was the dark suit and glasses, but he was alone. When he raised a hand and gave her a two-fingered wave, she waved back and smiled.

Suddenly, the lights dimmed even further to a smoky blue, and the beat of the music changed to something steamy and sultry. A spotlight captured the entrance of a woman at one end of a stage that jutted in a narrow line, halfway down the center of the room. She wore a midnight-blue dress that fell in a waterfall of sequined ribbons to the floor. The din of voices dimmed a bit, and, after a beat, she began to dance. Thigh-high slits in the dress revealed long, slender legs encased in fishnet stockings as she whirled one way and then the other. By the time the dancer had slithered around and up and down two of the aluminum poles that dotted the stage, Corie figured every eye in the house had shifted to the performer. Corie was so fascinated that she had a delayed reaction when Jack's hand grasped hers.

Just then the woman pulled some kind of snap and whipped the dress off. Beneath it she wore nothing but the fishnet stockings and a sequined thong. Corie blinked and looked again. It wasn't exactly a thong—no, it was more like a jockstrap!

She turned to Jack and gripped his hand like a lifeline. "She's a *he*."

Before Jack could reply, a man crawled up on the stage and tucked a bill into the strap. Corie's mind began to spin as quickly as the male dancer who was twirling around the poles again.

"Do you want to leave?" Jack asked.

"Are you kidding? We just got here." She leaned closer to be heard above the music. "Are the other women—" she waved a hand at the other tables "—really men?"

"Some of them."

Corie glanced around curiously. She felt as if she were at the eye doctor's office and he'd just slipped a more highly magnified lens in front of her eyes so that she could see everything more clearly. Was that woman sitting near Rollo a man? She was certainly big. But the woman at the table next to her was slender and fine-boned and the breasts that were under the spangled tube dress looked real enough. When the woman winked at her, Corie's eyes widened.

She was turning to ask Jack's opinion when the man who'd waved to her earlier pursed his lips and blew her a kiss. Smiling, she waved two fingers at him again.

Jack grabbed her hand. "Stop that."

"Why?"

"He's flirting with you."

"I know. I was trying to flirt right back. Wasn't I doing it right? He isn't a woman, is he?" She turned back to study him, and the moment their eyes met, the man rose from the table and started moving toward them.

"No, he's not a woman, and you were doing it fine," Jack gritted out.

"Watch out, sugar." The woman who'd winked at her earlier leaned closer. "He looks harmless enough, doesn't he?"

"Yes," Corie said.

"No." Jack spoke in unison with her.

The woman laughed. "Your boyfriend's right, sugar. Whatever you do, don't dance with him. His nickname's the Groper."

"May I have this dance?" the Groper asked.

"The lady's with me," Jack said, tightening his grip on Corie's hand.

"Sorry—"

"Shove off," Jack said.

"You tell him," the woman at the next table said.

Jack rose, and the man blinked behind his glasses and said in a whiny voice, "She waved at me. I thought—"

"You thought wrong," Jack said.

The man turned and hurried back to his table. Jack waited until the man was seated again, facing them, before he sat down and pulled Corie close. "I want to make sure he gets the message." Then he lowered his mouth to hers.

JACK KNEW THE KISS was a mistake the same way a rock climber knows he's taken the wrong step when the earth starts to crumble beneath his shoe. The moment that his mouth brushed against Corie's, he fell just that quickly, just that surely, but he couldn't have stopped himself.

If Corie had resisted or even hesitated, he might have been able to strap down the control that had been slipping away from him since he'd walked into that dressing room at Macy's. But she didn't resist. She didn't seem to believe in it, and he couldn't stop.

Her mouth was so soft, so pliant, her response so heated, so generous. His head began to spin. Already her taste was drugging him. The sweetness poured into him, reminding him of ice cream—the soft kind that melted instantly in the heat so you had to eat it fast.

He threaded one hand through her hair, then changed the slant of his lips on hers. With his other hand, he dragged her closer, pulling her to her knees on the banquette until she was nearly on his lap.

She still wasn't close enough to stop the ache that was building inside of him. Yes, he was used to having a woman cloud his senses. He was even used to having his blood heat, his body burn. But he'd never experienced this kind of razor-sharp need before. He wanted more.

In some far corner of his mind, he was aware that his hand had moved beneath her skirt. He felt the slide of cool, silky fabric on the top of his hand and the heat of smooth, impossibly soft skin beneath. It still wasn't enough to ease that knifelike ache that twisted inside of him. He needed more.

OH, PLEASE MORE. Corie wasn't sure whether she thought the words or murmured them against Jack's mouth. But the greed she was feeling now ran so deep that she didn't think it could ever be assuaged. She simply couldn't get enough of Jack's hungry kisses. His mouth was so soft, so warm, and when he slid his tongue against hers, he tasted like some dark, exotic treat that she'd been born to crave. Not even the most forbidden treats she'd ever indulged in had ever made her feel like this—like a river of electrical sparks was coursing through her body, right down to her toes.

No one should taste this good. Or feel this good. He was so hot. One of his hands burned like a brand on her thigh; the other was nearly raising blisters on the back of her neck. And his mouth was warm, firm and hungry on hers. But those three contact points weren't nearly enough. She wanted him to touch her everywhere. She needed him to ease the ache deep inside of her.

With one swift movement, she eased herself onto his lap so that she was straddling him.

"That'll be fifteen dollars." In Corie's mind, the voice seemed to come from far away. But Jack seemed to hear it perfectly well. He went still, and then he drew away and eased her back onto her knees on the banquette.

"Just a minute," he said, dropping his hand from the back of her neck and pulling a wallet out of his back pocket. Corie watched him draw the bill out with one hand and offer it to the waitress.

"Keep the change," Jack said.

"Thanks," the waitress replied. "Your friend Franco said he'd join you in a minute."

For a moment after the waitress left, neither one of them spoke. Corie's face was so close that Jack could see the separate spikes in her eyelashes. Her eyes were the dark green of the sea and he could see himself trapped in them. Trapped the same way his hand seemed to be caught beneath her skirt. He didn't seem to have the will to pull it free, any more than he had the will to push her away.

Dammit. All he wanted to do was kiss her again, and there were so many reasons why he shouldn't.

"Franco," she said, increasing the pressure of her hand against his chest.

"Franco?"

"She said he was on his way. We shouldn't have kissed. Franco might have seen us."

Jack's eyes narrowed. "Everybody in this place could have seen us kiss if they'd glanced this way. Why shouldn't Franco?"

"Because. I thought…I mean, aren't you and he…?"

"What?" Jack asked.

"I thought that you were…involved."

"Involved?" He'd always thought he was a man of few words, but Corie had a way of reducing him to one-word questions. And he was beginning to catch her drift. "*Involved?*"

"I thought you were a…couple." Then she frowned. "But if you were, then you probably wouldn't have kissed me quite that way, would you?" Pausing, she tore her gaze from his and glanced around the club. "Unless you…?" Letting her voice trail off, she glanced back at him. "I haven't had a lot of call to research stuff about sexual orientation in Fairview. Are you…do you…?"

He gripped her chin in his hand. "No to everything. And just so there's no possibility of a misunderstanding— Franco and I are just friends. I'm only into women, and I don't cross-dress."

"Oh."

Oh, indeed, Jack thought.

"I need to think about this," Corie said.

Well, he needed to think about it too. Kissing Corie Benjamin hadn't been part of the agenda he'd formed when he'd invited her to come to San Francisco. Now he wanted to do a lot more than kiss her.

"It might not be a good idea for you and me to become involved," Corie said.

Jack's eyes narrowed. She was one-hundred-percent right. In fact, she was only giving voice to the same thought that should have formed in his own mind. But it hadn't—not yet. And it ticked him off that she was saying it before he'd even had a chance to think it. "You can think about it all you want. But we're already involved."

She opened her mouth, but before she could say a word, he kissed her again. Although he managed to keep it brief, it took only that short, hard meeting of lips to bring back the heat and the incredible greed that he'd felt before. It didn't help one bit that her mouth parted eagerly, tempting him to sink even faster and further. But fear slivered through him. Because he knew he could lose himself in her. When he released her, they were both breathing hard and he wasn't sure just what he'd proven.

So there. Jack absolutely hated the fact that the adolescent taunt had formed in his mind. Now, he wasn't sure what to do next, but thankfully his cell phone rang.

He dropped his hand from the back of her neck to take it from his pocket and flip it open. "Yeah? You got something? Tell me."

When he felt Corie begin to move, he tightened his grip on her thigh. "Hold on a minute, Hawthorne."

"I'm going to the ladies' room," she said as she slid away from him and his hand slipped free of the skirt.

"You can't go alone," he said.

"I'll go with her," the woman at the next table said as she rose. "And I'll make sure that no one bothers her."

Jack frowned at the woman who now towered over Corie. "I don't think—"

"Reggie," Franco said, setting drinks down and then turning to embrace and air-kiss the woman. "If I'd seen you, I would have come over sooner. Have you met my friends Corie and Jack?"

"We were just about to introduce ourselves," Reggie said. "Tell your handsome friend here that Corie will be safe with me in the ladies' room."

Franco turned to Jack. "Reggie is a black belt in karate. Corie is in good hands."

Jack kept his gaze on the tall, buxom woman until both she and Corie disappeared into the crowd.

"She's a *he*, right?" Jack asked.

Franco smiled. "Last time I checked he was."

"What in hell were you thinking bringing Corie to a place like this?"

Franco raised both hands, palms out. "She wanted to experience San Francisco nightlife, and this is a very popular place."

"Don't give me that. You just wanted to see what kind of plot point you could get for that damn screenplay of yours."

"Moi?" Franco pressed a hand to his chest as he sank into the chair opposite Jack's. "Now you've hurt my feelings. Corie was very adamant about coming here. You heard her yourself at Macy's. After she saw the effect the man-magnet skirt had on Rollo, I think she wanted to really give it a whirl."

"The man-magnet skirt?"

"You know. I showed it to you. Marlo built a simply marvelous wardrobe around it."

Jack glanced in the direction Corie had gone. "She's wearing that skirt in a place like this?"

"Why not?"

Jack pinned Franco with a look. "I have business on the phone. When I'm done, you and I are going to talk."

And then he was going to have a talk with the little librarian.

CORIE TRIED TO SORT through her thoughts as she followed Reggie into the ladies' room. The lounge area of the rest room was empty, at least it was before two other women followed them through the door.

The first, a short, round brunette, breezed past them like a small tank, making a beeline for a plush red stool in front of the vanity that stretched across one wall. "My feet," she moaned as she slipped out of her shoes and wiggled her red-painted toes. "Thank heaven I don't have to wear these shoes every day."

"What a cru...u...ush." The tall, slender redhead had a dark-as-molasses voice, one she used to stretch the word into three syllables as she sauntered across the room.

"Who's your friend, Reggie?" the brunette asked as she fluffed her hair.

The redhead leaned against a wall and studied them.

"Corie, meet Sidney—" Reggie nodded at the brunette, then waved a graceful hand in the direction of the redhead "—and Morgan. Corie's a friend of Franco's."

Morgan paused in the act of powdering her nose to wiggle two fingers at Corie in the mirror. "Hi."

"Cha...armed." The redhead drew a pair of glasses out of her purse and slipped them on her nose. Peering through them, she smiled. "The better to see you with, my dear."

Corie studied the four images reflected in the mirror—

Sidney, a plump brunette in perpetual motion; Morgan, a redhead who didn't seem to move at all; and Reggie, a slender, buxom blonde with an easy smile that inspired trust. It was only as Reggie put a friendly arm around her and urged her closer to the vanity that Corie figured out she herself was the small blonde in the mirror.

Staring, she moved closer to her reflection. At least she'd been able to recognize the woman in the mirror at Macy's. But Corie didn't recognize this woman at all. Her cheeks were flushed. Her hair was mussed. Her bottom lip was swollen. Lifting her hand, she pressed her fingers to her lips. "Who am I?" she murmured.

Sidney laughed, a rich, hearty sound that filled the room. "Now, that's exactly what we were wondering, honey. Inquiring minds want to know."

"Knowing the competition is the key to success," Morgan drawled.

"Relax, girls," Reggie said, meeting their gazes in the mirror. "I don't think that Corie is in any competition with us. Are you, sugar?"

Narrowing her eyes, Corie studied the other three women as closely as they studied her. Could they possibly be...? "Are you...?" How did one put something like that delicately?

"We're men by day, sugar, if that's what you're asking," Reggie said as she sat down next to Sidney. "And what in the world is a nice girl like you doing in a place like this?"

"This is my first night in San Francisco and I wanted to go to a singles place where I could meet men," Corie said. "Franco brought me here."

Morgan's smile spread slowly. "We...e...ell, you sure enough came to the right city to go on a manhunt, girl-friend."

"And you've already met three of us," Reggie said, winking at her in the mirror. "Club Nuevo is a great place to look for a certain kind of man."

"I can see that." For the first time since she'd come into the rest room, Corie smiled.

"Now for the next big question," Reggie said, patting the chair next to her. "Why are you looking for a man when you came in with a hot one on your arm?"

"Jack and I—" Corie frowned as she sat down. "We... That is, I thought he was...gay. But he's not."

"And that's a problem because...?" Reggie asked the question, but Corie met three sets of curious eyes in the mirror. And wasn't it the same question she was asking herself?

"He's everything that my mother ever warned me about in a man," she finally said. Even to her own ears, the excuse sounded pathetic.

"The best ones always are," Morgan drawled.

"And if they're the type your mother forbade you to date, well, that just increases the temptation factor," Reggie said.

"Whoooeee! Does it ever." Sidney fanned herself with her hand.

"The question is do you want him for a fling or long-term?" Reggie asked.

"I'm only going to be in San Francisco for a week."

"Then I say go for it," Reggie said.

"Ditto," Sidney said.

Morgan nodded.

Corie frowned. "I'm not sure how to do that. I haven't had a lot of experience with men."

"Honey," Morgan said, her smile spreading slowly again, "men aren't all that hard to seduce."

"What she needs is a good strategy," Sidney said.

Corie met their gazes in the mirror. "Got any suggestions?"

Reggie's grin widened. "Does rain fall? My personal favorite is telling a man straight out what I have in mind. I paint the picture with words. A very vivid picture. Men are suckers for visual stimulation."

"Now me, I always go for temptation," Sidney said as she drew out her lipstick. "Just when I think he's interested, I back off and play a little hard to get. A man always wants what is just out of his reach. But, of course, I don't back off too far or too long." Sidney laughed, and the rich throaty sound filled the small room.

Three pairs of eyes met Morgan's in the mirror.

Morgan shrugged lazily. "I believe in conserving my energy for the important stuff. I say the next time you're alone with him, jump his bones."

Laughing, Reggie slapped her hand on the vanity. "Always a good backup plan."

"And if he gives you any trouble, I'm going to give you my card," Sidney said, whipping one out. "I've got connections in the D.A.'s office."

"Here's my card, too," said Morgan. "You want to sue his pants off, just give me a call."

Reggie drew a card out of her purse. "I don't have their clout or connections, but if you decide to dump him, I can offer you a little relaxation therapy. I work in this exclusive spa in Napa Valley. You just drop in anytime. I'll fit you in."

"Thanks," Corie said as she tucked cards into her purse. "And if I can ever do anything for you, just—"

"I thought you'd never ask," Reggie said with a grin. "I, for one, want to know where you got that skirt."

Corie beamed a smile at her. "I know someone who can tell you how to get a copy of it."

Sidney reached over to finger the hem. "Do they make it in big-girl sizes?"

JACK SLIPPED his cell phone back into his pocket and glanced in the direction of the rest rooms for the fifth time in as many minutes.

"She's fine," Franco said.

Jack knew it was true. He'd seen Rollo get up and follow Corie and her tall companion when they'd left the table. Plus, he'd overheard Franco talking to the doorman when they'd arrived. No one with dark glasses and a white cane would be allowed in the club. Corie was probably safer here than she would have been at the apartment building.

Except for the fact that he couldn't be sure that she was safe from *him.* He never should have kissed her. It had been bad enough to wonder what she would taste like. Now that he knew, he already wanted to kiss her again and more.

The question was what in the hell was he going to do about it? Oh, he could make a list of the reasons why he shouldn't want her—and right at the top was that she was the kind of woman who was looking for commitment in a man. More than that, she *deserved* commitment from a man. And that was the kind of woman he'd always avoided.

He glanced again toward the rest rooms. Unless he was very, very careful, he *was* going to kiss her again. Right now he was tempted to get up and...

He shifted his gaze to Franco. "What is taking her so long?"

"You know, I've never seen a woman affect you this way."

"What way?"

Franco studied Jack. "She rattles you. I've never seen a man with smoother moves than you have. Grabbing a woman and kissing her in a public place. That's not your style."

Tell me about it, Jack thought.

"With Corie, you act like you're not sure what your next move should even be."

Jack wasn't sure he liked being that transparent. He kept his gaze steady on his friend. "My next and only move is going to be to take her home."

Franco grinned and gave him a thumbs-up.

Jack's eyes narrowed. "It's not... I'm not...we're not." He couldn't believe he was actually stuttering.

"Whatever you say," Franco said. "Mum's the word. I won't mention it again."

"As soon as she gets back, we're leaving."

"Fine. But while we're waiting, tell me what you found out on the phone? Inquiring minds want to know."

"I should have a name and an address on my anonymous informant by morning."

"And then we'll go talk to him." Franco pulled his notebook out of his pocket.

Jack grabbed his hand. "So help me, if I see you write one more thing down in that notebook—"

Franco raised his free hand in a gesture of surrender. "Fine. You won't see the notebook again." Then he waved the hand he'd raised. "Corie's coming with her entourage."

Jack glanced in the direction that Franco was waving at and stared. Entourage was the right word. Britney Spears or Madonna might have a larger one, but certainly not one that was more eye-catching. He couldn't even see Corie at first. The person who called herself Reggie was in the lead, and he could just catch glimpses of Corie behind her, flanked by two other women, a tall redhead and a plump brunette. Rollo brought up the rear.

Jack rose when Corie introduced Morgan and Sidney. His announcement that they were leaving triggered a melee of hugs, air-kisses and "See you Saturdays" that lasted another five minutes. The moment they were out on the street, he took Corie's arm and pulled her to a dead stop. "What are you doing on Saturday?"

"Reggie and Sid and Morgan are going to take me to a different kind of singles place. They don't think I'm going to meet anyone here that's my type. Of course, they're going to wear more 'regular' clothes. Isn't that sweet of them?"

Jack gritted his teeth. It was an old habit that he'd broken years ago. "You are not going out alone with those three…men."

"Of course not." She beamed a smile at him. "They told me that you would insist on coming along. So, consider yourself invited."

THOUGH SHE HADN'T thought it possible, Corie was tired, deep-down bone-tired by the time Franco pulled his SUV into the parking area beneath his apartment building. The men had been quiet on the ride home, but as soon as they got out of the car, Franco said, "There are two ways to get into the building from here. That door right over there leads to a back stairway. Since you don't have a car, you'll probably use the front entrance, so we'll go that way."

Franco had barely finished speaking when the door he'd just pointed out opened. Both men stiffened, then relaxed as a young girl teetered toward them on really high platform sandals.

Franco pressed a hand to his breast. "Darcy, you scared us half to death."

Corie guessed Darcy's age to be about fourteen. Her hair was the shade Corie's had been pre-Lorenzo, but the girl wore hers long and straight with a few wispy strands hanging down over her cheek bones. The snug, threadbare jeans rode low on her hips, and the chartreuse tank top fit like a second skin, leaving her midriff and the rose tattoo near her navel bare.

She stopped in front of Franco with her hand outstretched. "You owe me fourteen dollars."

"Whoa!" Franco's brows shot up. "Don't think you can hose me, Darcy. We don't get that many packages delivered in a week."

Darcy cracked her gum and held her ground. "We had a deal. A dollar for every package I have to sign for when you're gone. And I counted fourteen in the delivery from Macy's. Plus, they came in a taxi, and I had to help the driver unload each one. Pay up."

"Not on your life. You only had to sign once for that delivery." Franco glanced at his watch. "Your mom won't be happy that you're up this late."

"It's not midnight yet." Darcy kept her hand right under Franco's nose. "The deal was one dollar for each package, not each package I signed for."

"Since they were my packages, I'll pay you the fourteen dollars," Corie said, fishing it out of her purse.

"Thanks." Darcy pocketed the money and fell in step beside Corie as Franco and Jack led the way out of the garage. "Are you with him?" She pointed toward Jack. "Or are you the latest addition to Franco's harem?"

Jack glanced back over his shoulder. "She's with me."

Corie pitched her voice low as she smiled at Darcy. "A harem?"

"That's what I call the women he rents his place to."

"I guess I'm part of it then. I'm a new tenant."

The girl smiled at her, and Corie noticed for the first time how really pretty she was. All she needed was a little help from Lorenzo.

"I'm kind of part of the harem, too. When my mom's out of town on business like she is right now, Franco keeps track of me. But it's not like he's baby-sitting or anything."

"Of course not," Corie said.

"Who's the big guy in the car?" Darcy asked.

Corie glanced to where Rollo had pulled into the driveway. "That's Rollo. He's sort of made himself my bodyguard."

"Cool. Are you a celebrity or something?"

"No. It's a long story," Corie said. The flagstone path they were on, cut sharply around the corner of the house, and she turned her attention to the two rows of old Victorian houses that faced each other down the length of the street. It was her first real look at the Painted Ladies that San Francisco was known for, and even in the dim light from the streetlamps, they were impressive. Scaffolding shrouded two of the old houses directly across the street.

"The place looks much better in the daylight," Franco said in a hushed voice.

"Does not," Darcy muttered under her breath.

"The two houses across the street are being worked on. The noise may bother you a little, but—"

"Save the tour for tomorrow, Franco. Corie's dead on her feet," Jack said.

And Jack was grumpy, Corie realized. He hadn't smiled or said much since she'd come back from the ladies' room with Reggie, Sid and Morgan. Maybe he was the one who was tired.

They'd just reached the second step from the top when Corie heard the dog yip. Turning, she saw a shadow emerge from the overhang of the scaffolding on the house directly across from Franco's. As it raced forward into the pool of light thrown by the streetlamp, she saw it was a small, fluffy dog. And she knew exactly where she'd seen it before.

"Get down." Grabbing Darcy's arm, Corie made herself a dead weight and dropped to the porch floor. Jack dropped with her, covering her body with his just as something whacked into the porch railing.

6

"DON'T MOVE." Jack spoke the words into Corie's ear.

Moving wasn't a possibility. Somehow she'd ended up face-down, sandwiched between Jack's body and the unforgiving boards of the porch floor. Next to her, she could just make out Franco and Darcy. Through the spokes in the railing, she spotted the small dog still huddled beneath the streetlight.

A loud noise split the silence. The dog streaked toward them and shot beneath the porch.

"Is someone shooting at us?" Darcy asked.

"No," Franco said, pointing through the spokes in the porch railing. "Look. It's Rollo to the rescue. He just fired a warning shot into the air."

Rollo stood at the side of his car, using the roof to support his gun arm. "Come out with your hands in the air," he said in a deep, gravelly voice.

There was no response. Then another noise, the roar of an engine springing to life, broke the silence. Corie spotted a car as it careened around a corner, backfired, then raced forward and lurched to a screeching halt at the curb across the street.

"Everyone, keep down," Jack said. "I'm calling 9-1-1." Corie felt him wiggle on top of her as he pulled out his cell phone. A second later, he was giving their address to an operator.

Across the street, a form shot out from the shadows beneath the scaffolding. Corie squinted her eyes, trying to get a better look as it streaked toward the car.

"Stop," Rollo shouted as he raced down the driveway. But he was too late. The figure across the street leapt into the front seat of the waiting vehicle, and the car peeled off down the street.

Rollo tore after it on foot.

"This scene is writing itself," Franco said. "Jack, you can strangle me later, but I need to get this down in my notebook."

"The police are on their way," Jack said.

Darcy got to her knees. "What is going on?"

Corie pushed at Jack. "Would you get off of me? They left the dog behind. He's under the porch. We have to get him."

"We're doing no such thing," Jack said.

"He's scared. Besides, he may have a tag with his owner's address."

"She's got a point," Franco said, scribbling away.

"Yeah." As Jack moved, he clamped a hand on Corie's arm. "Before we get the dog, I want to check something out." Rising, he leaned over and plucked an arrow out of the bottom rung of the railing. "It's got a note attached."

Opening it, he could just make out the words in the dim light: *You're in grave danger. Go back to Fairview.*

CORIE CAME AWAKE as she always did, suddenly and completely, like a diver shooting to the surface. But when she opened her eyes, the world around her was not the one she had awakened to for the past twenty-five years. The burgundy drapes and bedspread were clearly not the blue-flowered ones in her bedroom back in Fairview. Then the sight of the fluffy dog snoring softly on the pillow next to hers brought the events of the day before flooding back into her mind.

Quickly, she pinched her arm to see if she had dreamed everything. Neither the room nor the dog faded, but there was still one thing she had to check out. Slipping carefully from the bed, she moved to the mirror.

Sure enough, the new Corie Benjamin stared back at her. Relief streamed through her. She'd washed off the makeup—but the shorter blond hair still framed her face.

Yesterday—the most exciting and wonderful day in her life to date—had really happened. After fishing her notebook out of her duffel bag, she sank down into a nearby chair and flipped open to a new page. Then, for the first time in her life, she realized that she wasn't sure what to doodle. She didn't have to imagine an adventure because she was really having one. It was as if, after twenty-five years of living the same old predictable life, she'd stepped into an alternative universe—one where her dearest, most secret fantasies were coming true.

Of course, it would be better if someone wasn't trying to scare her into leaving San Francisco. But she didn't believe the man who'd shot the arrow at the porch had really been trying to hit her. No one who owned a shih tzu could be that mean.

Corie shifted her gaze to Horatio. That was the name on the tag that hung from the little dog's neck. She hadn't gotten a good enough look at the man who'd escaped in the car to tell for sure that it was the "blind" man from the airport, but Jack said the police had identified the airport dog as a shih tzu. And Horatio was definitely that. When she was ten, she'd researched a lot of small dogs in an attempt to convince her mother to let her have one, but Isabella had been frightened of animals—even a little powder-puff breed like a shih tzu. Corie had felt a kinship for Horatio from the moment Jack had coaxed him out from beneath the porch and handed him to her. And the dog had felt a definite kinship for her. He'd refused to let anyone else hold him.

Slowly, she drew a line across the blank page in her notebook. Of course, Jack did have a point about the "blind" gunman who had switched to arrows—he might be trying to scare her away for a good reason. But until she found out what that reason was, it wasn't good enough to keep her from finding the answers to her questions.

Quickly, she drew a cluster of stick figures—the Lewises. Any hope she had of being welcomed by them was quickly fading since they were the most likely suspects behind the warnings. Who else would care if she came to San Francisco? So much for that fantasy.

But Jack Kincaid was another fantasy altogether. Ever since he'd kissed her, he'd become the very best part of her alternate universe. Just thinking about the kiss brought back that melting warmth and zing of excitement that she had experienced when Jack had pressed his mouth to hers.

With a sigh, Corie set down her notebook. The problem was, how was she going to get him to do it again? Once they'd left Club Nuevo, he certainly hadn't given any indication that he even *remembered* kissing her. There'd been nothing loverlike in the way he'd crushed her beneath him on the porch. That had been about protecting her, and he'd been all business when he'd dealt with the police who'd responded to the 9-1-1 call.

Rollo had gotten a partial license plate, but even after the police had left, Jack had kept his distance from her, letting Franco give her a tour of the apartment while he checked to make sure the windows and the door to the balcony were all locked.

He could have lingered after Franco had finished the tour. If he had, she might have had the courage to try one of the strategies that Reggie and Sid and Morgan had suggested. And she might have ended up with a man in her bed instead of a dog. And not just any man. It was Jack Kincaid she wanted in her bed.

Blinking in surprise, Corie rose and took another look at herself in the mirror. More than her hair color had changed. She felt very different from the woman who'd stood in Fairview a few days ago, staring into another mirror.

Had it started at Lorenzo's? Or had it happened when she'd put on the skirt that Franco had given her?

She raised a hand and touched her lips. Jack's kiss had certainly contributed to her metamorphosis. She'd never fantasized about actually getting a man into her bed before. Oh, she'd had sex, but neither of the two lovers in her past had actually been in *her bed.* There was something...more permanent about that.

Corie heard a symphony of warning bells going off in her mind. Jack Kincaid was *not* the kind of man a girl should have permanent thoughts about. He was an adventure, the type of man with whom with a girl had a once-in-a-lifetime fling.

She had six more days in San Francisco, and that was just about the right time frame for a man like Jack. She was going to be in deep trouble if she didn't remember that.

Suddenly, she frowned. She wasn't going to have a fling, six days or otherwise, if she didn't choose a strategy and put it to use. Soon.

A sharp yip from Horatio had her whirling away from the mirror. He stood at the foot of the bed, his tail wagging frantically, and yipped again.

"I bet I know what you want," she said as she rummaged through her duffel and pulled on her running shorts, shoes and a T-shirt. The moment she lifted Horatio from the bed, he began to wiggle his way out of her arms, and when she set him on the floor, he raced for the door. "I know, I know. Nature calls. Let's see if we can find a back way out of this place."

Walking the dog would give her a chance to think.

Dear Mrs. H,

I'm writing because I simply can't wait another minute to give you another update on my latest screenplay. Things are happening at breakneck speed. Think *Sopranos* meets *My Fair Lady*. That is what is known in the screen trade as a very high-concept idea. And it's a dangerous one, too. In the past twenty-four hours, my heroine has been shot at twice, first by a bullet and then by an arrow. And the shooter is a blind and possibly mob-connected hit man whose sidekick is a fluffy little shih tzu. I couldn't think up stuff like this!

In addition, I've transformed a little wallflower into A-1 date bait.

Best of all, I think the skirt has already hooked my little fair lady up with her true love. The first time my friend Jack saw the little librarian in the skirt, it was like watching Cupid's arrow hit a bull's-eye. And if he even suspected that he was beginning to fall, he'd head for the hills. The guy's had real commitment problems since his aunt died when he was eighteen. But that's another story.

Let's just say that the skirt is taking San Francisco by storm. Three "ladies" from one of my favorite clubs are going to be ordering copies of it even as I'm writing this!

The urban legend continues to grow! Give my best to Pierre and to all my friends at the Willoughby.
Ta,

Franco

THE MOMENT Corie stepped outside the house, she saw Jack. He was doing some sort of exercise on a small flagstone patio.

Naked from the waist up, wearing only gray sweatpants, he leaned forward, walking his hands along the ground until his body formed a *V*. Then slowly, he lowered himself inch by inch, until his body hovered a bare inch above the flagstones, supported only by his hands and his toes.

Muscles corded along his shoulders and arms. Sweat gleamed over every inch of his exposed skin. Corie felt her mouth go suddenly dry, and once again she experienced a primal need to touch him. To run her hands over those slick, hard muscles. And then to taste him.

She would have gone to him right then if her feet had been able to take orders from her brain. But her legs had turned to jelly, and she was almost sure she could feel her brain following suit.

Drawing in a deep breath, she watched Jack raise his head and arch his back slowly. The muscles in his neck corded and she thought she might die from wanting to bite him right there.

Think. Plan, she reminded herself. The girls had given her a lot of advice in the rest room at the Club Nuevo. Sidney's idea of tempting him by backing off and playing hard to get was out since Jack had already backed off. On the other hand, Morgan's strategy of jumping his bones—although it was exactly what she wanted to do—was out because jelly legs just couldn't jump.

So she was left with Reggie's plan—to tell him straight out what she wanted. Paint a picture. And she would. In a minute, she was going to march over there and tell Jack Kincaid just what she'd like to do to him.

JACK COUNTED the beats as he drew in air and let it out. Balancing his weight on his feet and one hand, he turned his body and stretched his other hand to the sky. Then he filled his lungs with air and exhaled. When he couldn't run, Yoga breathing exercises were the one foolproof way to clear his mind. But they weren't working. Corie Benjamin had filled his dreams all night long and he couldn't rid his mind of her even now.

If he'd been worried about her safety, that would have been one thing. But protecting her hadn't played a big part in the fantasies that had woven their way into his dreams. She'd stirred something inside of him, a hunger that he couldn't seem to tamp down. And that frightened him.

Bringing his hand down to the ground, he shifted his balance again and concentrated on his breathing. In and then out. In and then out. Perhaps *frightened* was too strong a word. *Worried* was more accurate. Under other circumstances and with another woman, the solution would be easy. He would simply make love to her and get her out of his system that way. Just thinking about the possibility of making love to Corie tightened his body and he had to shift a foot to keep his balance.

For a moment, Jack concentrated solely on his breathing. Then he began his exercise again. Making love to Corie Benjamin was *not* a good solution. She deserved better than a man who was using her to get information that might put her newly found father in jail.

Then there was the fact that until they figured out who was after her and how to stop them, he had to devote all his energy—24-7—to keeping her safe. And that included keeping her safe from him.

The best solution to the problem was to make sure he kept his distance. With Rollo standing guard outside and Franco on duty in the house, she should be perfectly safe in that upstairs apartment for the time being, and that would free him to check out the person who was e-mailing him once Hawthorne arrived and gave him an address.

Walking his hands to his feet, Jack straightened, then grabbed a towel and wiped his face. He caught movement out of the corner of his eye, and whirled to find Corie approaching him across the grass. For a moment, he thought he might have conjured her up out of his fantasies. Then the dog yipped sharply.

CORIE STILL WASN'T SURE how she'd managed to walk. Perhaps it was a case of hard-core lust winning out over jelly legs. Whatever the reason, she had an even bigger problem now. Reggie's method seemed simple on the surface—just tell the man what you want. Paint a word picture. But how in the world did one go about it? Should she just blurt it out? Or should she do a little prep work first? *Hi, Jack, nice day. How about some wild, hot sex?*

Would she even be able to speak? Up close the gleaming wet expanse of skin affected her even more potently than it had from a distance, and she was suddenly aware of his scent—sunshine, sweat and something very male. It had wrapped around her, so that every breath she drew in was Jack. If she could just keep her eyes on his face, she might be able to gather her thoughts. But her gaze seemed to have become magnetized to a drop of water that was slowly winding its way down his chest. When it finally disappeared beneath the waistband of his sweatpants, her throat went bone-dry.

"What are you doing here?" Jack asked.

Staring. That's what she was doing, and her imagination had kicked into overdrive, picturing what might happen if she had the courage to go to him now and follow the path that drop of water had taken with her hand, or her tongue. She had never before felt this kind of need to touch a man. Or taste him. The temperature, which had been warm when she'd stepped out the door with Horatio, shot up several degrees.

"I thought..." In a minute she was going to be able to speak coherently. But first she had to get her eyes off the waistband of his pants. Dragging her gaze up to meet his, she said, "Horatio needed to come out. And you said we'd talk in the morning."

"Talk? Yeah."

Narrowing her eyes, she studied him and for the first time noticed that he looked a little dazed. His knuckles were almost white where he was gripping his towel. Could he possibly be feeling even a fraction of what she was feeling? The possibility gave her courage. *Tell the man exactly what you want.* Reggie's words became a little chant in her head.

She cleared her throat. "I'd like to have sex with you."

For a moment the words hung between them. Reggie had said to paint a vivid picture, and one was certainly forming in her mind. She could see the two of them wrapped around each other, rolling across the patio. But Jack wasn't moving—not even a muscle. She dropped her gaze to his mouth. His lips had thinned into a grim line. They wouldn't be as soft as they'd been last night. They would be hard and demanding. A little thrill shot through her right down to her toes.

Corie licked her own lips and then drew in a deep breath. *Vivid* is the word Reggie had used. Perhaps Jack needed more specifics. "I want to taste you—your mouth, your skin." She lowered her gaze down his chest to the waistband of his sweatpants. "And then..."

"Corie—" The word sounded as if it had been torn out of him. "Oh, hell!" He moved toward her.

She had a second to prepare, to anticipate, before his hands gripped her upper arms and his mouth closed over hers. But nothing could have prepared her for the high-voltage sensations that slapped into her.

This. At last this. The kiss was even better, more potent, than the one they'd shared at Club Nuevo. It felt like the time she poked her finger into a live socket—only it was her whole body this time. And she could feel everything— the slick, smooth heat of his skin beneath her hands, the way his muscles tensed and hardened. She heard the sharp intake of his breath when she pressed her body against his. And when his tongue at last tangled with hers, she could taste anger, and, beneath that, the deep, ripe flavor of passion that might have been her own.

Greed shot through her, sharp and edgy. She wanted to devour him. No, she wanted to get so close that she could disappear right into him.

HE COULDN'T GET enough of her. Each time he touched her, the realization that he might never get enough of her became clearer. This time the sharp spurt of fear was quickly lost in the other sensations pouring through him. He could feel everything—the movement of her lips beneath his, a vibration of sound. She'd said something. His name? He couldn't make it out over the thunder of his heart.

He shouldn't be doing this. In the one sane part of his mind that wasn't filled with her, he knew that. But when he'd seen her standing there, when she said she'd wanted to have sex with him, he'd had to kiss her again. Control. He was a man who'd always prided himself on it, but it was slipping away. Fear came again in a stronger wave, and this time it was pushed away by greed.

He had to get closer...until she melted into every part of him. He had to touch her. Moving quickly, he backed her across the flagstones and braced her against the glass door of the patio. Then he ran his hands over the soft cloud of her hair, the delicate curve of her throat. Unable to resist, he lowered his mouth and sampled that soft neck. When her pulse fluttered against his lips, he scraped his teeth over it and felt the tremor move through her. He had to have more.

This time when she moaned his name, he heard it, and the sound of it had his needs building, escalating, spinning out of control. Pressing her more firmly against the glass door, he ran his hands over her, this time in possession. He found her mouth again and devoured.

SHE WAS DROWNING at the same time that she was burning up in the heat. Glorious waves of it radiated through them, between them. If her body hadn't been pressed against his, if his hands hadn't been on her, Corie was sure she would have dissolved right onto the floor.

And that's where he would take her—where they would take each other. Just as she'd pictured it. The two of them rolling, legs tangled, and finally joined, here and now on the flagstone patio, splashed with sunlight. It would be wonderful, wild...

She felt a slap of cold the moment Jack stepped back from her. Head spinning, she stared at him. If she'd had one ounce of strength in her arms or in her legs, she would have reached out to him and dragged him back. But he'd weakened her. It was as if he'd taken some vital part of her with him. When he took another step away, she began to tremble.

JACK WAS THE FIRST to speak. "I'm sorry."

"Why?" She was trembling.

"Because...we can't." Drawing in a deep breath, he smelled only her. He wanted to go to her, but if he touched her again, he was horribly afraid that he might start trembling, too.

"I thought you wanted what I wanted."

"I did." He was still close enough that he could see himself trapped in the cloudy green of her eyes. They reminded him of the ocean when it was stirred up by an approaching storm. He wanted very much to dive right back in.

Taking another quick step back, he stumbled into the wrought-iron table, then quickly moved behind it. Perhaps if he put something between them... "I did want to kiss you. But...what I meant to say is that I...I..."

Dammit. He was stuttering again. In another minute he'd be babbling. No other woman had ever made him babble. But she looked so stricken. How in hell was he supposed to say the right thing when his head was still spinning?

Taking in a deep breath, he tried again. "I'm sorry. We shouldn't. We can't." There. He'd come full circle without making any sense at all. But the words had to be his mantra. *We can't. We can't.* Latching on to them, he hoped and prayed that he could convince himself.

"Why not?" Corie asked.

Did she have any idea how thin his control was? How close he was to throwing aside the table and grabbing her again? "Because someone is trying to hurt you."

"No." She shook her head.

"A bullet. An arrow. What is it going to take to convince you?"

She lifted her chin. "He's just trying to scare me away. The bullet went into the air, and the arrow carried a message."

"And when he learns that you don't scare easily? What do you think he'll do then?"

"He still won't hurt me."

"Corie—"

"No," she raised a hand to stop him, "Let me finish. He owns a shih tzu. I did a lot of research on dogs when I was a kid." She waved a hand at Horatio who was seated nearby on the flagstones, thumping his tail. "That dog wouldn't harm a flea, and research shows that dog owners are very much like the breed they choose."

Jack glanced at the dog, then drew in a deep breath. There was only one way he could think of to make her take the attacks seriously. "Look, it's understandable that you don't want to think ill of a man that you believe might be your father. But there's something I haven't told you."

"Okay, tell me."

"Coffee first." He was going to need it. Moving toward her, he opened the door and led the way into his apartment.

Once inside, Jack distanced himself from Corie by moving behind the kitchen counter. He set the teakettle on to boil and took his time grinding beans and measuring them into the French press pot. But even as he focused his attention on the ritual of making the coffee, he was aware of her wandering around the small living room, the dog at her heels. The little thing had taken to her on sight. Hell, he'd taken to her himself on sight.

And now he was going to hurt her. He'd seen the expression on her face when he'd shown her that picture of Benny and her mother. Jack poured boiling water into the pot. He knew only too well what it was like to want a family—and lose it. Now, he was going to tell her that a man she believed was her father might have been responsible for his aunt's disappearance.

But she was so sure that she wasn't in any real danger. He had no choice but to warn her. Resolved, he turned. She was standing in the center of his living room, the light pouring through the window haloing her hair, and desire hit him again like a hard fist in the gut.

"You haven't lived here long."

It took him a moment to realize she'd spoken and another for the words to register. "No. How do you know that?"

"You haven't accumulated any junk. Except for the folder on your desk, this room is as neat as a hotel room."

"You're very observant," Jack said.

She shrugged as she moved to the counter. "I'm curious. My mother always said it would be my downfall."

His lips curved slightly as he plunged down the press on the coffeepot. "My aunt used to say it would be my downfall, too."

"She doesn't say it anymore?"

Jack drew in a deep breath. "She disappeared twelve years ago. She's probably dead, and I'm pretty sure that Benny Lewis had a hand in it."

Corie moved quickly around the counter, and before Jack could even anticipate it, she had wrapped her arms around him and laid her head on his chest. "I'm so sorry."

For a moment Jack couldn't move. He'd thought he'd known what her reaction would be—shock, disbelief and perhaps even anger. Why was it that she could always surprise him?

"It's hard to lose someone you love," she said.

And she would know exactly how hard. He wasn't even aware that he'd wrapped his arms around her. All he knew was that it felt right. He couldn't remember the last time he'd held a woman like this. Had he ever? What he was feeling was so different from when he'd held her pressed up against the door earlier or when he'd had her on his lap at the Club Nuevo. The fire that he'd felt moments ago had been replaced by a sweetness and warmth that streamed through him. He didn't want to let her go. That realization made him draw away slightly, but he kept his arms around her.

"Did you hear what I said, Corie? I think Benny may have had my aunt killed."

Corie met his eyes steadily. "Do you have any proof?"

"No. The official report listed her as a missing person. She was working as the Lewis family's personal chef on the estate at the time. I'd just gone away to college. I was all the family she had. She was all that I had. She wouldn't have just gone off without telling me."

"Why do you suspect Benny?"

"About a week before she disappeared, she called me at school. She was worried about something she'd overheard, but she wouldn't tell me what. She said that she was going to check into it and then she'd tell me all about it. I was busy, excited about being in New York. I didn't even think about it much until she disappeared."

"Did you tell the police?"

"Oh, yeah. But they didn't pay much attention. They thought I was a crazed, grief-stricken eighteen-year-old. That was the spin the Lewis family was putting on my suspicions and accusations."

"That must have been hard."

No one had understood that at the time. Not D.C. and

not even Franco, who had flown out from New York with him. Jack felt something inside of him melt and stream away. At the same moment, he dropped his arms and took a step back. "I intend to find out what happened. I'm sure that there's something going on out there at the winery, something that Benny is determined to hide. My aunt found out about it and she had to be eliminated. I won't stop until I find out the truth."

"I don't blame you. What can I do to help?"

Jack stared at her. "I don't understand you. I'm telling you that I convinced you to come out here so that I could use you to put your father in jail, and you're not angry. Plus, you want to help."

"I'm not the wide-eyed innocent that you seem to think I am. And I didn't come out here with any stars in my eyes about my long-lost family welcoming me with open arms. My mother 'disappeared' twenty-six years ago. Something frightened her enough that she ran and she didn't ever contact Benny or anyone in his family. Over the years, she wrote hundreds of letters to Benny, but she never mailed them. I don't intend to be like my mother. I'm going to meet Benny Lewis and find out what happened. I want to know what turned her into a recluse and why she was so determined to turn me into one, too. So, are we partners?"

Jack reached for the coffeepot and poured two cups. After he'd taken a swallow, he said, "My conversations with you never go where I expect them to go. I thought when I told you about my aunt, you'd be scared enough to hole up here until the party Friday night."

"No way. I broke a promise to my mother when I came out here. I intend to make use of every minute." She held out her hand. "Besides, two heads are always better than one. Do we work together or not?"

Jack hesitated for a moment, then took her hand. "I

don't know exactly how it worked in the old *Thin Man* movies. In our case, I'm the senior partner."

She had her mouth open—Jack was sure she was about to object—but the ringing of the phone stopped her.

"I have to get that," Jack said as he moved toward the door to the bedroom. "The police may have something on that license plate."

CORIE BREATHED a little sigh of relief as she watched Jack disappear into the bedroom. At least he'd agreed to a partnership. She could almost hear Morgan's voice in her ear, drawling, "Follow him, sugar. You'll never have a better chance to jump his bones."

But she didn't quite have the nerve to try it. Maybe she hadn't changed as much as she thought she had.

She picked up her coffee and carried it with her into the other room. Still, she'd held her own with Jack. He'd agreed to let her work with him. And pitting her wits against him was almost as stimulating as kissing him.

Just thinking about kissing Jack made her knees turn into jelly again. What would it be like to make love with him? She sank into the chair at Jack's desk. She had definitely changed. The Corie Benjamin who lived in Fairview didn't have her mind filled with images of rolling around a patio with a man. And with Jack, she wanted to do a lot more than think about it.

A whine from Horatio had her glancing down at the floor. Leaning over, she scooped him up. "You got any pointers?"

Horatio licked her face eagerly.

"You agree with Morgan then." Glancing at the door to the bedroom, she thought about it. She could hear the rumble of his voice as he spoke on the phone. If she went to him right now and he rejected her again, she'd only have Sidney's strategy to fall back on.

"Later," she promised herself. That way she'd have two strategies left. That would give her more confidence. As Horatio settled himself on her lap, her gaze dropped to the papers spread out on Jack's desk. Along one side of them were some photographs, and she recognized one of them as Benny.

He was older and even more handsome than in the photo with her mother. After hesitating for a minute, she ran her finger along the man's cheek.

When she felt Jack's presence in the room, she glanced up. "It's just a picture, and yet I can see why my mother was attracted to him."

"He has a great deal of charisma. My aunt was running a very successful restaurant in the city when he decided he wanted her for his personal chef."

Corie set the picture aside and picked up the next one. The woman was young with blond hair and blue eyes. "Who is this?"

Jack moved closer to the desk. "That was Benny's wife, Bianca. She died shortly after the twins were born."

Corie picked up the next photo. The woman was as dark as Bianca was fair, and there was none of the fragility that was so apparent in Bianca.

"That's Rose," Jack said, "Bianca's older sister. She came to help with the children after Bianca died. For years, she ran the house. When the twins went away to college, she created the spa and now she runs that part of the family business."

Corie hesitated before she picked up the last photo. It was a group photo—two younger men stood with Benny and another man. There was a strong family resemblance between all four of them. "And these are my half brothers," she said, pointing to the younger men.

"Yes. They both work in the winery, and they do well enough that Benny leaves them pretty much in charge. He's been spending more and more time at the vineyard he bought in Italy."

Corie studied Benny's two handsome sons. The photo had been taken from a distance, and it was hard to make out their features. But they were smiling at the camera with an easiness that made her want to smile right back. "I knew about them from reading your article, but seeing them makes them more...real." She looked up and met Jack's eyes. "I'd like to meet them."

"If they know about you, they might each have strong reasons for wanting to scare you off," Jack said.

"I know. I'd still like to meet them." She tapped her finger on the fourth man in the picture. "Who's this?"

"That's Buddy Lewis, Benny's older brother. He's always been kind of a misfit on the business side of things. They let him run some of the tours, and he's active in community and volunteer groups. When my aunt worked there, he was heavily involved in a local theater group and sat on a board to promote tourism in the valley."

She replaced the photo where she'd found it. "Why do I have to wait until Friday? Why can't we just go out to the winery and take a tour?"

"Not on your life. We're not going anywhere until we get a better handle on who's trying to scare you off," Jack said. "D.C. hasn't been able to trace the owner of the dog, but I'm expecting some news on my anonymous e-mailer at any minute, so I'm going to change. While I'm doing that, why don't you read the file and get better acquainted with your family?"

Corie glanced at him in surprise. "You'd let me do that?"

"Sure." He smiled at her. It was the first real smile that Jack had given her—ever—and she felt it right down to her toes. "You're my junior partner, aren't you?"

As she watched him disappear into the bedroom again, Corie thought again of her mother's commandment. When Jack Kincaid smiled that smile, he could probably convince a woman to do anything he wanted.

Horatio yipped, scrambled down from her lap and raced toward the door. Corie could see Darcy standing outside the screen. Rising, she followed Horatio. "Hi. You're up early."

"My mom called to check on me during a work break. It's already midmorning in New York." Darcy pushed her fingers into the front pockets of her jeans. "She has to travel a lot." Her tank top was white today, and the rose tattoo was still clearly exposed. "Are you going to be renting Franco's apartment for long?"

"I'm not sure."

The girl was lonely. Corie had experienced the feeling enough herself to recognize it. At least her own mother had worked at home. "Jack fixed coffee. Would you like some?"

"Sure." Darcy's face brightened. "My mom lets me drink it as long as I put a lot of milk in it."

Corie mixed a half-and-half mixture of coffee and milk, then carried it out to the patio. "I had the same deal with my mom until I went away to college. How did you manage to get yours to agree to the tattoo?"

"Are you kidding? She didn't. It's one of those paste-on ones."

The moment Darcy plopped into a chair, Horatio ambled over to sniff her shoes, then licked her toes.

"I think he likes the black polish," Corie said.

Darcy glanced up from the dog. "I'd be happy to help you out with taking care of him—if you want."

"That would be great. How about if I pay you whatever Franco does?"

"Sure." The girl's face brightened again as she leaned down to pet the dog.

"Did you tell your mom about the man who shot the arrow last night?" Corie asked.

Darcy shook her head. "If I did, she'd be breaking her lease so fast. With the traveling and everything, she has a real thing about making sure I'm safe and all. While she's gone, she depends on Franco to watch out for me. He makes sure I keep to my curfew and everything. My shrink says my mother's extraprotective because my father sued her for custody when I was eleven. She's still afraid he'll pull something like that again. I can't even go out and hang with my friends when she's out of town. I'm stuck here."

For a moment, Corie wondered what it might have felt like to have a father who cared that much for her. Had her mother been worried about Benny suing for custody? Was that why she ran away? "My mother always insisted that I stay close to home, too. It got boring."

Darcy smiled at her. "It's been a lot more fun since Franco started renting out his apartment to all these women." She leaned closer. "Did he give you the skirt to wear?"

"Yes," Corie said. It was the first time since she'd woken up that she'd remembered the skirt. Would she have been more successful with Jack if she'd been wearing it?

"There have been a lot of men hanging around since Franco brought that skirt here," Darcy said. "I asked him if I could wear it, but—"

As if on cue, the screen door to Jack's apartment opened and Franco stepped through it. "I told you that you were too young."

Franco's outfit, the bright crimson kimono in combination with the lime-green sunglasses and matching high-top sneakers, had Corie blinking her eyes.

He was carrying a pot of coffee on a tray. "I made a fresh pot. Anyone for refills?"

Suddenly they heard an irritated voice. "Let go of me. I'm working for Jack Kincaid."

Rollo appeared around the side of the house with a scrawny young man in tow.

"I've got a friend who's a cop," the boy muttered, digging in his heels and trying to jerk his arm free. "He'll vouch for me."

Rollo's grip remained firm. "This young man says he's here to see Jack Kincaid. Can any of you vouch for him?"

"Never seen him before," Franco said, frowning at the boy. Then he turned his head in the direction of the screen door and yelled, "Jack, you have company."

Corie studied the boy. She guessed him to be about fifteen, and judging from the piercings, just about up to his eyebrows in parental rebellion.

"Hawthorne," Jack said as he stepped out onto the patio. Then he crossed to the boy and extended his hand. "You've got news?"

"Yeah."

"Good. I have another job for you."

Rollo released Hawthorne's arm. "I frisked him. He's clean."

"Thanks," Jack said, and then shook hands with the boy. "We had a shooting incident last night, so we're taking precautions. I don't have any pizza, but how about some coffee?"

"Yeah."

"Sure."

Hawthorne and Rollo spoke in unison, then glanced at each other.

"No hard feelings?" Rollo asked.

"Nah," Hawthorne said. "I been frisked before."

"Really?" Darcy asked.

Hawthorne shrugged. "A few times."

Darcy studied him. "Have you ever been in jail?"

"Almost. My father made a few phone calls and saved my butt."

"I think my mom would leave me there to rot," Darcy responded.

"Here you go." Franco passed out mugs to Hawthorne and Rollo. He pitched his voice low as he offered a mug to Corie. "Looks like those two are hitting it off."

Jack waited until Franco had served everyone and Rollo had returned to his station at the front of the house before he spoke to Hawthorne. "Have you got my e-mailer?"

Hawthorne nodded. "The bill for the e-mail account is mailed to a business called the Saratoga Grill. The name on the account is Edie Brannigan. The grill is five miles south of Calistoga near the Lewis Wineries. I have the address."

"I know that name," Corie said.

Jack turned to her. "How?"

"My mother had an old menu from a place called Edie's Diner. I did some research and found out it changed its name to the Saratoga Grill about five years ago."

"Edie's Diner," Franco repeated the name with a frown. "Wait a minute. You know the place too, don't you, Jack? Didn't we all go there after that memorial service the Lewises held for your aunt?"

"Yeah," Jack said. "I know the place, and I'm going to pay a little visit to the owner."

"And I'm going with you, partner," Corie said.

Franco whipped his notebook out and beamed a smile at the two teenagers. "What we have here is a clue and a major plot point! Way to go, Hawthorne!"

7

JACK TOOK THE CORNER QUICK, cut around a van and pressed his foot on the gas pedal. The top was down, Mozart was flowing out of the stereo speakers and the sun was pouring down. Under any other circumstances he would have been enjoying the challenge of zigging and zagging through San Francisco traffic, but he wasn't. Reason number one was that he was making sure that he wasn't being tailed.

Reason number two was sitting in the seat next to him, looking as if she didn't have anything more to worry about than Horatio, who was presently perched with his hind legs on her lap and his nose poking out the window as far as he could get it. They were on their way to the Saratoga Grill, formerly known as Edie's Diner to talk to the person who'd been sending him anonymous e-mails. The fact that Corie's mother had saved an old menu from the diner indicated that someone there might know something about both Isabella Benjamin and Corie. Why had they kept silent all of these years? And why break that silence now? Those were the questions that were spinning around in his mind.

The only sign that Corie Benjamin was experiencing any of the tension he was feeling was the whiteness of her knuckles on the hand that was gripping the dog's collar. He jerked his attention back to the road because he'd started to notice other things, too. The skinny little T-shirt she was wearing left an inch of midriff bare, and the skirt inched higher on her thighs every time he glanced over.

His plans for keeping his hands off of his junior partner had pretty much been destroyed. He'd come very close to taking her right on his patio without much thought as to where they were. It was the second time that she'd made him lose track of where they were. As often as he might tell himself that he wasn't going to touch her again, he knew now that it was a lie. He didn't make a habit of lying to himself.

A sharp blast of a horn had him reining in his thoughts and focusing on the traffic. At the next corner, he shot into the far left lane and took a quick, sharp turn into oncoming traffic. Tires squealed and horns blared, but as he slammed his foot hard on the gas pedal, he was pretty sure no one would be able to follow until the light turned again. The car shot through the next intersection and over the crest of a hill.

"This is what they do in every San Francisco car chase scene," Corie said. "Except we didn't bounce up in the air before we started down the hill. Why not?"

"We'd have to be going faster, and I'd rather not leave my transmission behind."

Her laugh had him glancing at her again. He had just enough time to see her whole face lit with excitement before he jerked his gaze back to the road. Even then, he could feel the energy radiating from her. It was a tangible thing in the car. Yesterday, she'd reminded him of Eliza Doolittle getting her first glimpse of Henry Higgins's world. Today, she reminded him of Alice on her first day in Wonderland.

Alice was a much better analogy, he decided. Because she was every bit as curious and prone to finding trouble around every corner. Agreeing to a partnership had been a mistake. If he hadn't, he might have been able to persuade her to stay at the apartment with Franco. But the words had slipped out before he could think to prevent them.

An even bigger problem was that, even though she would have been safer back at the apartment, he'd wanted her to be with him. He simply wanted *her*—in a different way than he'd ever wanted any other woman. The intensity of his desire was one surprise. His inability to keep control of it was another.

"You surprise me," Corie said.

That made two of them, Jack thought as he shot her another glance. Horatio leaned a little farther out of the window, and as she reached to ease him back, her T-shirt inched up a little further. When the dog settled on her lap, the skirt inched up even more. Each time he looked at her, it became harder and harder to transfer his gaze back to the road. He was even finding it difficult to remember that they might have a tail. Glancing in the rearview mirror, he took a quick right and headed away from his destination— the Golden Gate Bridge.

"Okay, I'll bite. Why do I surprise you?" he asked.

"I didn't take you for a Mozart-and-flutes kind of man. And I never would have pictured you sulking."

"I'm not sulking."

"The corners of your mouth are turned down. You've barely spoken to me since we left the apartment. If it looks like a duck and quacks like a duck…"

He couldn't prevent a grin. "I'm not sulking. I just wish you'd take the shooting stuff a little more seriously."

She ran a hand down Horatio. "I do take it seriously. I know that someone is trying to scare me away. I also know that I'm not going to let them. Maybe that means I'm like my father."

The pride in her voice had him glancing at her again.

"Maybe you are. My aunt always thought he was a man of true courage."

"Really?"

"He uprooted his family and moved across a continent because he wanted to build a different kind of life for them. She admired that. I did too when I believed it."

"But you don't anymore?"

He frowned. "I believe parts of it. No one can argue with what Benny Lewis tried to do and the success he's made of his business. But something was going on at that winery, and when my aunt poked her nose into it, she disappeared."

Corie reached over and placed her hand briefly on his. "We'll find out what happened. We know who was sending you the e-mails, and Hawthorne says he's sure he can track down Horatio's owner. We're making progress."

For a moment, Jack didn't say anything. Just that short contact, the brush of her hand on his, had been enough to have some of his tension easing. And they *were* making progress. D.C. hadn't been able to come up with a name for Horatio's owner yet. So, when they'd left the apartment, Hawthorne had been engaged in Lord knew how many illegal activities on Jack's computer while Darcy was heating up whatever frozen pizzas her mom had left in the freezer. Franco had been reluctantly sitting in the living room reviewing his screenplay notes while some kind of rap music—chosen by the teenagers, of course—had been blasting out of the stereo. Jack didn't envy Franco.

Turning left at the next corner, Jack headed toward the bridge and the Napa Valley. Rollo had taken a different route, but he would rejoin them at the bridge.

"If it's any consolation, you surprise me, too," he said.

"Really? How?"

We'd like to send you 2 FREE BOOKS and a surprise gift to introduce you to Harlequin Temptation®. Accept our special offer today and

Live the emotion™

HOW TO QUALIFY:

1. With a coin, carefully scratch off the silver area on the card at right to see what we have for you—**2 FREE BOOKS** and a **FREE GIFT**—ALL YOURS! ALL **FREE!**

2. Send back the card and you'll receive two brand-new Harlequin Temptation® novels. These books have a cover price of $4.25 each in the U.S. and $4.99 each in Canada, but they are yours to keep absolutely free!

3. There's no catch. You're under no obligation to buy anything. We charge nothing—ZERO—for your first shipment and you don't have to make any minimum number of purchases—not even one!

4. The fact is, thousands of readers enjoy receiving books by mail from the Harlequin Reader Service® Program. They enjoy the convenience of home delivery...they like getting the best new novels at discount prices, BEFORE they're available in stores...and they love their *Heart to Heart* subscriber newsletter featuring author news, horoscopes, recipes, book reviews and much more!

5. We hope that after receiving your free books you'll want to remain a subscriber. But the choice is yours—to continue or cancel, any time at all. So why not take us up on our invitation with no risk of any kind. You'll be glad you did!

GET A *Free* MYSTERY GIFT...

We can't tell you what it is...but we're sure you'll like it! A FREE gift just for giving the Harlequin Reader Service® Program a try!

Visit us online at
www.eHarlequin.com

Your FREE Gifts include:

- 2 Harlequin Temptation® books!
- An exciting mystery gift!

HARLEQUIN®
Live the emotion™

Scratch off
the silver area to see what the Harlequin Reader Service® Program has for you.

YES! I have scratched off the silver area above. Please send me the **2 FREE BOOKS** and gift for which I qualify. I understand I am under no obligation to purchase any books, as explained on the back and on the opposite page.

342 HDL DU4C   142 HDL DU4S

FIRST NAME	LAST NAME

ADDRESS

APT.#	CITY

STATE/PROV.	ZIP/POSTAL CODE

(H-T-07/03)

THE HARLEQUIN READER SERVICE® PROGRAM—Here's how it works:

Accepting your 2 free books and mystery gift places you under no obligation to buy anything. You may keep the books and gift and return the shipping statement marked "cancel." If you do not cancel, about a month later we'll send you 4 additional books and bill you just $3.57 each in the U.S., or $4.24 each in Canada, plus 25¢ shipping and handling per book and applicable taxes if any.* That's the complete price and — compared to cover prices of $4.25 in the U.S. and $4.99 in Canada — it's quite a bargain! You may cancel at any time, but if you choose to continue, every month we'll send you 4 more books, which you may either purchase at the discount price or return to us and cancel your subscription.

*Terms and prices subject to change without notice. Sales tax applicable in N.Y. Canadian residents will be charged applicable provincial taxes and GST.

She sounded and looked so pleased that Jack had to smile. "I never figured you'd be so stubborn."

She laughed. The sound blended well with the Mozart and flutes. "My biggest flaw. Right after being curious and impulsive. My mother always predicted that my flaws would lead to my tragic downfall. She even came up with three commandments to keep me on the straight and narrow."

Curious himself, he glanced at her again. "What were they?"

"Never trust a charming man, never act on impulse and be careful what you wish for."

"I'd say that's pretty good advice."

"Yeah—if you want to live the life of a nun. That's the kind of life my mother led, and I've decided it's not for me."

"What kind of a life do you want?"

Corie leaned back against the seat. "I haven't figured it all out yet. For so long, I've just wanted to do more than live in Fairview and go to the college every day. Not that I don't like my work. I do. Books, research, working with the students—I loved it. I do love it. But I just want more. I want to see things for myself. My mother never understood that."

Jack understood it all too well. "My aunt wanted to keep me close to home, too. She wanted me to stay in California for college. Stanford was every bit as good, maybe better, than NYU. But I wanted to get away, see the world. We argued, but I went anyway." It was the first time in his life that he could recall his aunt being unhappy with him. "If I hadn't left, she never would have taken the job with the Lewises. I think she did it because she didn't want to live alone. If I'd gone to Stanford, she might be alive today."

Now, where had that come from? He'd never spoken about the argument or the guilt he'd felt over it to anyone.

Corie reached out and covered his hand on the wheel. "You had nothing to do with her disappearance. Bad things just happen. We can't control them."

Hadn't he told himself that thousands of times? Somehow, just hearing her say it made the tightness in his chest loosen.

"If you'd stayed here, would you have been happy?" Corie asked.

Jack pictured what his life might have been like if he'd never left San Francisco. "No, I wouldn't have been happy."

"Your aunt wouldn't have been happy then either, I bet." Suddenly, she craned her neck to look back at the street they'd just passed. "The bridge. I saw it."

And he hadn't. Releasing her fingers, Jack put his hand back on the wheel and eased the car around the next corner. For a minute there, he'd forgotten completely that they had a destination and an urgent reason for getting there. The Saratoga Grill was still an hour or more away. As he approached the bridge, he eased the car into the far right lane. In the rearview mirror, he saw Rollo pull in behind them.

He glanced at Corie. She was leaning forward in the seat as far as the belt would allow. "Drive over it as slowly as you can. I want to savor every moment."

He eased his foot off the gas pedal.

"There isn't any fog today. I so wanted to see the bridge disappear in the fog. I read all about it—the scientific reasons for it."

"The best view is from the Marin headlands. The fog moves in at ten to twenty miles per hour and even the tall spires become cloaked in it. You'll forget all about the science and swear it's magic."

"Look."

Jack glanced in the direction she was pointing and saw a large cargo ship cut a white path through the water. Alcatraz lay just beyond it. "You'll have to take the tour of the 'Rock,'" he said. In his mind, he could picture her on the boat with the wind whipping at her hair. "It's not required by law, but almost every tourist seems to feel obligated to go there. When we get this shooting thing all sorted out, I'd like to show you the city."

She beamed a smile at him. "I'd like that."

He was usually careful with words. He knew the power that they carried, and he always preferred to think before he spoke. Around Corie, he'd developed a habit of speaking before the thought had fully formed in his head. But he did want to show her San Francisco and see it through her eyes. Ignoring the warning voice in his head, he assured himself that if he spent time with her, he might be able to figure out how to get more control over his feelings.

Of course, the other alternative would be to provide the affair she seemed determined to have. The idea had slipped so easily into his mind—as if it had been patiently biding its time like a skilled thief, waiting for the moment a security system was most vulnerable. And now that the thought was there, Jack knew that he would have a hell of a time pushing it aside again.

CORIE FELT her stomach knot as Jack pulled into the parking lot across the street from the Saratoga Grill. The emotions—excitement, fear, longing—had been building steadily in her as they'd driven north through the Napa Valley.

This was it. She was going to find out something about

her mother and possibly her father. She pressed a hand against her stomach.

"It's not too late," Jack said. "We can go back to San Francisco and do this another time."

"No. I just—" When she broke off, he was silent, but his hand covered the one she'd fisted on her lap. She hadn't expected understanding, and she felt some of her tension ease. "I'm not a coward."

"I should say not. You're one of the bravest women I know."

She turned to meet his eyes. "Really?"

He smiled at her. "A coward would be back in Fairview by now."

Corie felt something warm bloom inside of her.

"I've got an idea." Jack pulled an ice cream on a stick out of the brown paper bag he'd carried out of the convenience store they'd just stopped at. "My aunt used to say that there wasn't anything in the world that couldn't be made better with ice cream."

"My mom used to say that junk food would clog my arteries."

"Please." Jack's tone was aggrieved. "There's nothing on the ingredients label that I can't pronounce. This is premium stuff. Do you have any idea what they charge for it?"

Corie had a very good idea. She'd been at his side when the man who ran the gas station and convenience store at the edge of town had rung up the total. While Jack had chosen some candy and lingered over the selection of ice creams, he'd struck up a conversation with the man behind the counter. That was when Corie had learned close up how a good investigative reporter collected his information.

By the time they'd left the store, Jack had learned all

about how Edie Brannigan's granddaughter and grand-son-in-law had enlarged the diner, created a patio for garden dining and hired some of the brightest new chefs from the local culinary institute.

"Okay," Jack said with a sigh. "If you can't eat the whole thing by yourself without breaking every health food rule you've been raised by, we'll share it. That way it's half the sin, right?"

Corie watched him open the box and take a bite. He didn't chew it. Instead, he let the ice cream melt on his tongue. Long moments ticked by before he swallowed and licked his lips.

"Now it's your turn."

The ice-cream bar was inches from her lips, the crisp chocolate coating broken and the creamy vanilla exposed, but she wasn't thinking of the ice cream when she opened her mouth and took a bite. She was thinking of tasting Jack, of what it had felt like when he'd kissed her, the slow, sure and easy brush of his tongue against hers. There was a look in his eyes that told her he knew exactly what was going on in her mind.

"Feel better now?" Jack asked as he reached over to rub the pad of his thumb over the corner of her mouth. For one second, she was intensely aware of the icy sensation of the ice cream and the heat of his hand.

Oh, she felt better—right down to her toes. And she wanted very much to feel better still. To lean closer until she completely closed the distance between them, to lose herself in the bright rush of sensations that he could bring her.

The dog stirred and sighed on her lap and as she dragged her gaze away from Jack's, she reminded herself of what she should be focusing on—finding out who owned Horatio and why he was determined to scare her away from San Francisco. Edie Brannigan might very well have the answers to their questions.

"You're worried that you'll find out something that you don't want to know."

"It's partly that." Corie stroked a hand over the sleeping dog. "Do you ever get a case of the nerves when you're tracking down a story?"

"All the time."

She blinked and turned to stare at him. Passionate, brooding, angry, frustrated. She could picture him in all those moods. But she couldn't quite imagine Jack Kincaid being nervous.

He laughed and urged her to take another bite of ice cream. "You should see your face. You're sure I'm lying through my teeth."

She might have denied it, but she found her mouth full of ice cream.

"You don't drop in for an impromptu interview with one of the warring tribal leaders in Rwanda without a major attack of nerves."

Swallowing, she asked, "What do you do when you don't have any ice cream to settle them?"

He grinned at her. "I keep my mind on the story. Following leads, gathering all the facts, finding the truth that lies beneath. That's what's fascinated me ever since I can remember."

"Yes." She glanced back at the diner. "Me, too. That's why I became a librarian. This isn't so much different, is it? I just want to find out the truth about why my mother had to run away to Ohio."

"It's a little different when the truth you're after is personal. But you're not alone. We're going in there together," he said as he tucked the now bare ice-cream stick into its box and disposed of it in the trash bag hanging from the glove compartment.

"All set?" Jack asked.

"Yes." Unbuckling her seat belt, Corie opened the door and got out. Horatio yawned, then yipped as she set him on the gravel at her feet. The opening of a car door and the crunch of gravel had her turning, and she noticed for the first time that Rollo had pulled up behind them in the parking lot. She handed Horatio's leash to him and Jack handed him the bag of goodies from the convenience store. They'd decided earlier that Rollo would baby-sit Horatio and keep an eye out for anyone suspicious while they were in the diner.

"Let's go," Jack said, holding out his hand.

The gesture warmed her. But it wouldn't do at all to let herself lean too much on Jack Kincaid. "What's your plan?"

The look he gave her held bafflement. "I don't have one except to go in there, order some coffee and see what develops."

"Same strategy as the convenience store. It was a pleasure to see you in action."

This time it was amusement she saw in his expression. "Honey, I didn't have a plan in the convenience store. I just went in and played it by ear." He squeezed her hand. "I have an idea that field research is a lot different than the kind you do in libraries. Usually the only concrete plan I have is to watch my back."

Not a bad idea, Corie thought as they walked through the door of the diner. The interior was cool in sharp contrast to the sunlight that was pouring through the wall of windows. A narrow counter ran the length of one of the walls and booths filled the other. A scratchy version of "Blueberry Hill" flowed out of the jukebox.

Though the hour was late for breakfast and still early for lunch, two tables were filled. The occupants had glanced up when she and Jack had entered. The two elderly gentlemen at the rear returned to their game of chess. But the two younger men seemed to have frozen in place with their forks poised over a mountain of French fries. The intensity of their gaze had Corie running a hand down her skirt to make sure it hadn't ridden up her legs.

"I just made a fresh pot of coffee. Interested?"

Corie turned her attention to the woman behind the counter who smiled and waved them forward. She could still feel the gaze of the two men as she moved with Jack to the counter and sat down.

"You read my mind," Jack said.

It wasn't until the woman whose name tag read Sabrina had placed mugs and a pitcher of cream in front of them that Corie realized she was still clutching Jack's hand. Feeling foolish, she let it go and picked up a spoon to stir cream into her coffee.

Something had changed. Corie gave Jack a sideways glance as he laughed at something Sabrina said. He wasn't just the man she wanted to have an affair with anymore. Nor was he merely her ticket to finding answers about her parents. Somehow, over the duration of the car ride through the Napa Valley, he'd become someone she could talk to and lean on. She hadn't had someone to share her feelings with for a very long time—not since she'd become a teenager and begun to clash with her mother.

Taking a sip of her coffee, Corie studied him in profile over the rim of her mug. He chatted as easily with the pretty woman behind the counter as he had with the man at the convenience store, and he was drawing her out in the same subtle, clever way. In less than three minutes of "playing it by ear," he'd found out that Sabrina was Edie Brannigan's granddaughter.

Corie picked up her spoon and stirred her coffee again while she continued to study him. It was easier to be objective when he was focused on someone else, and she didn't have to look into those eyes or face that dimple head-on.

One thing hadn't changed. She still wanted him, perhaps even more than she had before. But it was different now. Nerves knotted in her stomach again. Frowning, she stirred her coffee faster while she considered her options. She could pull back now and accept the easy friendship he seemed to be offering.

Or she could risk a lot more than a nervous stomach and try to seduce him again. She was beginning to think that an affair of any length with Jack Kincaid was going to leave her with a huge dent in her heart.

Wasn't that what she was beginning to suspect had happened to her mother?

On the other hand, even if she returned to Fairview with a dent, wouldn't that be better than living a life just dreaming about a man like Jack?

Or writing love letters that you were afraid to mail?

"You stir that coffee anymore, and you might wear a hole in the bottom of the cup."

Twisting on her stool, Corie saw that one of the young men from the booth had slid onto the stool next to her. The other was hovering right behind him. They were both lean and dark, and handsome when they smiled. Brothers, she guessed. The resemblance between them was strong.

"I'm Joey and the shy one behind me is Frank," the one on the stool said. Then he leaned closer to Corie. "Frank wants to ask you if you and he haven't met somewhere before."

Sabrina snorted. "That's the best line you came up with?"

"I told Frank that it sounded like a line," Joey said. "But, honest, he really thinks he knows you from somewhere."

Corie couldn't prevent a smile. The odd thing was that the two men looked a little familiar to her, too. "I can't remember meeting either one of you before."

"Ouch. Well, maybe we've just run into you somewhere? Frank wants to know if you're from around here."

Frank punched Joey in the shoulder. "I can speak for myself."

Joey leaned closer to Corie and spoke confidentially. "You wouldn't want to listen to him. We're twins, and he's the evil one."

Twins. Suddenly, the memory that had been tickling the edges of her mind slipped into place. She'd seen these men before in the pictures that Jack had shown her. They'd been younger then, but the resemblance to their father was clear. These two men could very well be her half brothers.

Corie didn't know that Jack had taken her hand again until he squeezed it. "The lady is not from around here."

Frank's eyes narrowed when they shifted to Jack. After a moment, he frowned. "Hey. I know you. You're that reporter from the *Chronicle*—Jack Kincaid."

"Guilty," Jack said.

"Shoot," Joey said, his smile fading until he shifted his gaze back to Corie. "We were going to offer the two of you a deluxe tour of the Lewis Winery. Frank was going to do the honors himself. But we can't invite your friend. He's not allowed on the estate." He slipped a card out of his pocket and handed it to her. "But you can come sometime if you want. It would be a pleasure. Frank and I noticed you the moment you came in here. Now, when was the last time we let anything distract us from our breakfast, Sabrina?"

"It was before my time." Leaning closer to Corie, she spoke in a confidential tone. "It usually takes a small explosion to deflect those two from the breakfast special."

Joey rose from his stool. "Anytime you want that tour, you just give us a call."

Frank nodded at her as he moved past. "Sooner or later, I'm going to figure out where I saw you before."

Corie found she couldn't talk. All she could do was stare as the two men left the diner. They were funny and handsome, and they could be her half brothers. She'd thought she was prepared, but—

When Sabrina moved down the counter to greet another customer, Jack squeezed her hand. "Are you all right?"

"Yes."

He tucked a strand of hair behind her ear, and without thinking she leaned into his hand. "Do you think that they knew my mother and that's why I look familiar to them?"

"Could be. On the other hand, with the way your legs look in that skirt, I'd be tempted to try the old 'haven't we met before?' line myself."

She smiled. "I can't imagine you saying anything that trite."

"Those Lewis boys are harmless," Sabrina said as she topped off their coffee. "But I've never seen them act that way before. They seemed really taken with you."

"Have you known them long?" Corie asked.

"Ever since I can remember. They've been sneaking down here for breakfast ever since they were little. Their mom died when they were little tykes, and their Aunt Rose raised them. She's the one who runs the Crystal Water Spa up the road, and she had strict rules about their diets when they were young."

Jack's hand still covered hers, and the strength of it, the warmth of it, had her gathering herself together.

Sabrina gave a little laugh. "Grandma says that before the boys could manage it on their own, their Uncle Buddy brought them here whenever he could sneak them out."

"You know, the last time I was in here was before the renovations. Edie was still pouring the coffee," Jack said. "She was a great listener. Does she come in at all anymore?"

"Sure does. Grandma comes in every day for the breakfast shift," Sabrina said. "Then she goes out back and putters in the garden until I give her a call to help out with lunch."

"Would she mind some company?" Jack asked.

"She loves company. Just follow the path that begins at the edge of the patio."

Corie waited until Jack had paid the bill and they were outside the diner on the sidewalk. Then she squeezed Jack's hand and said, "I'm glad you're here."

FOR A MOMENT Jack said nothing. He couldn't, not when he was swamped with the emotions that those four little words had triggered. He was standing on a sidewalk in the bright sunlight, but he had the strangest sensation that he was sinking into deep waters and the woman standing in front of him was his only lifeline.

When she'd leaned her cheek against his hand in the diner, he'd wanted to simply carry her off. Right now, he wanted to gather her close and hold her. Somehow he didn't think either of those techniques would give her what she needed right now. Her hand was gripping his like a vise. She'd just met two men who were probably her half brothers, blood relatives she'd spent a lifetime not knowing. That had to be hard, and what she learned from

Edie might be harder still. What she needed now was a little distraction.

Smiling, he said, "I'm beginning to think that Franco was right about the powers of that skirt."

"What do you mean?" There was surprise in her eyes, and curiosity—just what he'd hoped for.

"The skirt. Franco says it has a strange effect on men. I didn't believe him, but it sure seemed to charm Joey and Frank."

"I guess it did." She drew in a deep breath and let it out. "They're nice."

"Yeah. I liked them, too."

This time it was a mixture of pleasure and relief that flooded her eyes. "I'm glad. And I've got an open invitation to tour the estate, with Frank as my tour guide." She glanced down. "Maybe there is something about this skirt."

Jack followed the direction of her gaze and frowned. The thing was halfway up her thighs. Not that he'd minded that much when he was the only one enjoying it. "There's something all right. It's too short."

She smiled at him. "Actually, given its effect, I'd say it's just the right length." Keeping his hand tucked tightly in hers, she drew him with her around the side of the building. "Let's go try our luck with Edie, shall we?"

THE WOMAN WAS TALL, thin as a rail with white hair pulled into a ballerina's knot at the nape of her neck. Her glasses had slipped down to the very tip of her nose, and she was peering through them, totally focused on pruning leaves off a plant that had grown thick over a trellis.

"Ms. Brannigan," Jack said.

"Just a minute. Every time I turn my back on this ivy, it goes wild."

Saying no more, Jack and Corie stopped when they were still a few feet away. Edie Brannigan continued to snip leaves while one minute stretched into two and then three. Finally, she set down her shears. "Thank you," she said as she stood back to study her handiwork. "I don't like being yammered at when I'm working." She took off her gardening gloves, dropped them into a nearby basket and turned to them, pushing her glasses up on her nose. "What can I do for—" Pausing, she pressed her hand against her chest. "You."

Jack moved toward her, and taking her arm, urged her toward a glider. "Why don't we sit down?"

"I'm fine. I just wasn't expecting—"

"Can I get you some water? Or should I call your granddaughter?" Jack asked.

Stiffening her shoulders, she shot him a look. "Stop fussing. Didn't I tell you I was fine?" Then she pushed her glasses up her nose and studied Corie more closely. "Well, you look like your mother. The hair's a different color. Hers was darker, but your eyes are the same." She held out a hand. "Come here and sit with me, child."

"You knew my mother, then?" Corie asked as she sat down next to the older woman and took her hand.

"Yes." Then she frowned and turned to Jack. "Why did you bring her here? Didn't you get my last message? You should have taken her back to Fairview."

"I tried to talk her into going back, but she wouldn't."

Edie snorted. "Talking won't do any good when action is required. I expected more of you."

"You can't blame Jack for the fact that I'm still here," Corie said.

Edie shot a frown at Corie. "And why not? I can blame whomever I choose. It was a free world the last time I looked."

"She's right, Corie," Jack put in. "I haven't—"

"You keep out of this, young man." Edie spared him another look. "I'm discussing this with Isabella's daughter." Then she turned back to Corie. "Why didn't you go back?"

"I came out here to find out if Benny Lewis is my father and why my mother ran away from him. I'm not going home without answers."

Edie threw back her head and laughed. "You're a lot spunkier than your mother."

Oh, she *was* spunky all right, Jack thought as he leaned against one of the columns in the arbor. And frustrating and unpredictable, and…fascinating.

She'd just defended him to a rather intimidating old woman. That one simple fact had a tumble of other emotions running through him. As far as he could recall, his aunt was the only other woman who'd felt compelled to race to his defense.

"You even sound like your mother," Edie said.

"Did you know her very well?" Corie said.

Edie nodded. "She worked in the diner for six months, and she rented a room from me upstairs."

As Edie continued to talk, Jack found himself watching the play of dappled sunlight on Corie's features. She was tense. He could see it in the stiffness of her shoulders and in the way she was gripping her hands on her lap. He thought of Joan of Arc, braced to face her enemies. She was scared to death about what she might learn. But she wasn't going to let that stop her. She wasn't going to let anything stop her from learning about her mother, her family.

Admiration and something he couldn't put a name to moved through him as he made his way to stand behind the two women. The moment he put his hand on Corie's shoulder, he felt some of the tension there ease.

"She'd lost her parents the year before in a fire that had

destroyed their tailoring business," Edie said. "Isabella had a bit of insurance money, and she was determined to add to that until she could go to college. One day about four months after she started working at the diner, Benny came in to fetch his sons. They were here with their Uncle Buddy, and when he saw Isabella with the boys, it was love at first sight. They met regularly here in the gardens at first, but it wasn't long before Benny took her to the house and introduced her to the rest of the family. His wife Bianca had only been dead a year. And Benny had been grieving. I don't think that anyone expected him to remarry so soon, but he and your mother were definitely making wedding plans."

"Then what happened?" Corie asked. "Why did she run away to Ohio?"

Edie leaned closer and spoke in a hushed voice. "Your mother was taken into the witness protection program."

Jack tightened his grip on Corie's shoulder. "What are you saying? Did she see something or overhear something when she was with the Lewis family that put her life in danger?"

"Now hold on just a minute," Edie said. "I can only tell you what Isabella told me, and she never did tell me the whole story. All I know is that, one weekend, she went to San Francisco with Buddy and Rose and the boys, and *poof!* She never came back."

"Did you report her disappearance to the police?" Corie asked.

"Oh, the Lewises did that. Benny was beside himself. He even hired private investigators. The boys had been teasing Isabella for weeks, begging her to take them on a boat trip. They were dying to see Alcatraz. So she talked Benny into making it a family outing. Benny got sick at the last minute and couldn't go, so Rose and Buddy went with them instead."

"What happened?" Jack asked.

"No one knows for sure. There were several rumors," Edie said with a glance at Corie. "The fog was rolling in when the tour boat left Alcatraz. Buddy always maintained that she must have taken a misstep on the deck and fallen overboard. There was also some talk that she committed suicide. The police found a note in her apartment, saying she was sorry—and that she couldn't take the pressure of the boys and running the estate. Garbage. All of it! I told them she didn't write it."

"Everyone thought she committed suicide?" Corie asked.

"No, not everyone. There was another more vicious rumor that she had another lover and ran away with him. Benny was fifteen years her senior, and an age difference like that always causes speculation. Supposedly, she was afraid of Benny and left the suicide note to keep him from looking for her."

"Do you believe that she had another lover besides Benny?" Corie asked.

Edie patted Corie's hand. "Good heavens, no, child. Not Isabella. I never could understand why someone would start a rumor like that."

But what if it was true? Corie didn't know what to make of the thoughts spinning around in her head. Her mother had never told her about being in the witness protection program, and she'd steadfastly refused to tell her anything about her father. *Never trust a charming man.* What if there was another charming man besides Benny?

"When did Isabella first get in touch with you?" Jack asked.

"About eight months after she disappeared, I got a letter

from her, telling me that Corie was born. She apologized for not getting in touch with me sooner, but she wanted me to know that she wasn't dead. That was when she told me she'd been taken into the witness protection program and swore me to secrecy. She said that in order to protect Corie, she had to stay hidden away for the rest of her life."

Edie turned to Corie again. "Once a year on your birthday, she'd send me a letter with pictures and an update on her life. The postmarks were all different. She told me she arranged to have truckers who stopped at a nearby diner take them and mail them from different cities."

"When did she finally tell you where we lived?" Corie asked.

"She didn't," Edie said.

Corie frowned. "Then how did you know that she died? How could you tell Jack where to find me?"

Edie sighed. "I got an e-mail a month or so ago. I don't know who sent it. You can't tell when the return address is just a bunch of numbers. But whoever it was knew a lot about your mother and you. He—or it could have been a she—anyway, he knew about the witness protection program and he knew exactly when your mother passed away. Told me how to access the obituary online so that I could see it for myself. He encouraged me to get in touch with Jack Kincaid."

She shifted her gaze to Jack. "He told me that you would know if it was safe to contact Corie. I knew something about you, so I thought it would be all right." She looked back at Corie. "I hope I made the right decision."

Corie patted the older woman's hand. "You did."

"You have no idea who e-mailed you?" Jack asked.

"No."

"Can I look at the e-mails?" Jack asked.

"Sure. I can't see the harm in that," Edie said. "My laptop is right over here in the cottage. I saved all the messages."

Jack moved around the bench to take Edie's arm and help her rise from the bench.

"Well, your manners are pretty enough," Edie said. "Your aunt did a good job on you."

Jack's eyes narrowed. "You knew my aunt?"

"She used to come in the diner when she worked for the Lewises." Whatever else Edie might have said was interrupted by the sharp barking of a dog, punctuated by bellowing shouts.

"You come back here, you little—"

Horatio burst into view on the path with Rollo in close pursuit.

"Horatio, what is it?" Corie asked, scooping up the dog when he reached her.

The moment she lifted him, he lapped her face, then whined once, and settled on her lap.

"Good heavens, I've never seen Horatio settle like that for anyone except for Buddy and Benny."

"You know Horatio?" Jack asked.

Edie continued to stare in amazement at the dog. "I see him practically every day. That's Benny Lewis's dog."

8

CORIE GLANCED DOWN at the doodles she'd been drawing in the small notebook on her lap. In the center of the page was a thick, brick wall. On either side of it, she'd sketched two stick figures banging their heads against the bricks. The one with the skirt, she labeled Corie, and the one with no skirt, she labeled Jack. The picture captured her current frustration perfectly. Too bad it wasn't animated.

"Order another pizza, Franco," Jack was saying. "Hawthorne is a growing boy." Corie glanced over to where he was pacing beneath the arbor, his cell phone pressed against his ear. He'd been on it ever since Edie had gone into the restaurant to help with the lunch shift. From what she could gather, Hawthorne was now working on tracing the anonymous e-mails that Edie had been receiving.

At her feet, Horatio sighed deeply in his sleep.

"Exactly," Corie said as she drew a stick dog on her pad. She leaned against the back of the bench. Her head was still spinning, even more so since they'd talked to Edie. She should be thinking, but it was hard when her emotions were so close to the surface. Every time they discovered a clue, it seemed to lead either nowhere or to more questions. And sometimes the answers weren't what she wanted.

Corie closed her eyes. She'd come to San Francisco to find out why her mother had hidden away in her house all her life. Now that she knew, she wanted to know what had happened to force her mother to go into the witness protection program in the first place. What part had Benny Lewis played in it? And perhaps most important of all, who was pulling the strings in all of this?

She hadn't realized just how much she'd wanted Benny to be her father until now when she had to face the possibility that he wasn't. And if he wasn't, who was?

Straightening, she set her notebook down on the bench beside her and glanced at Jack again. He'd been pacing back and forth beneath the arbor, badgering a slew of people he'd called on his cell phone for the past hour. From what she could gather from his intermittent three-word sentences, he wasn't getting any further than she'd gotten by doodling in her notebook.

Hawthorne had confirmed what Edie had told them, Benny Lewis was indeed Horatio's legal owner. But the dog was very attached to Buddy, too. Odds were that one of them was the shooter. Corie thought of Jack's description of Buddy as the family misfit—the only one of the Lewises who didn't have a job description. According to Sabrina, Buddy was the kind uncle who used to bring Joey and Frank to the diner for the kind of food that their Aunt Rose wouldn't allow them to have. Edie put the odds at 10 to 1 against Buddy being the shooter. The man was in his seventies and as kind a person as you'd like to meet.

But Benny was out of the country. He couldn't possibly be shooting at her. Could he? Corie pressed a hand against her temple to stop the spinning.

"D.C., I know you've got friends at the bureau. Yeah, I understand that the witness protection files are kept secret. Right. They don't even exist. But this was twenty-six years ago. The woman they were protecting is dead, and now someone is shooting at her daughter."

Jack had just run into another brick wall. Corie glanced

down at her sketch. But they were going to break through that wall because Jack Kincaid wasn't going to give up until he got answers. The man was a regular bloodhound.

"What's it worth to me?" Jack laughed. "How about your next day off we go out on the boat? And one more thing...can you check with the local police? Someone had to have investigated Isabella Corinna's disappearance all those years ago. See if you can find out who worked the case. And they've got to have a copy of the supposed suicide note. Okay, *two* days on the boat. I'll hold."

He was grinning as his gaze shifted to Corie's and held. "You okay?"

She nodded.

"We're going to figure this out."

Corie didn't doubt that. What she couldn't quite figure out was what she was going to do about Jack Kincaid. Just looking at him standing there in the dappled sunlight made her want to go to him and simply hold on. It wasn't merely the grin and the dimple in his chin that hit her like a blow to the stomach. It was the whole package. Jack Kincaid was incredibly competent, loyal to his friends and honest. And she wanted him for much more than a fling.

"You're not going back to Franco's," Jack said. "I'm going to get you a room at my friend Jake Monahan's hotel. He has first-rate security, and you'll be safer there than at Franco's."

Corie's stomach sank. He hadn't said *we*. He'd said you're not going back to Franco's. What kind of advice would Reggie, Sidney and Morgan have for seducing a man long-distance? Phone sex?

"Yeah, I'm still here, D.C. Tell me you've got good news."

She was banging her head against a wall on more than one front. Frowning, she began to pleat the hem of her skirt. The problem was that the whole idea of seducing Jack Kincaid was beginning to intimidate her a bit. Not that she was having second thoughts—not at all. It was just that having a fling in theory was a lot easier than seducing one particular man in reality, especially when nothing she'd done so far had worked.

He seemed to be immune to the skirt. She smoothed out the pleats she'd made, then slipped her fingers beneath the hem and rubbed it between her fingers. It certainly felt like an ordinary skirt. But Franco swore it had powers, and she'd certainly witnessed its effect on Rollo. And something had caught Joey and Frank's attention in the diner. Horatio heaved a huge sigh at her feet. According to Edie, Horatio had never taken to a woman before, not even Rose who lived in the same house with Benny. Every male she came in contact with was affected by the skirt, except for the one man she wanted it to affect.

Suddenly, her fingers stilled on the hem of the skirt. Jack was looking at her. Corie knew because she could feel the heat of his gaze right through her clothes. The moment she raised her eyes to meet his, desire twisted hard inside of her, and for the first time in her life she knew what it was to crave.

D.C.'s VOICE had become a buzz in his ears. Jack tried but couldn't seem to absorb any meaning from the words. Nor could he take his eyes off of Corie. Something had drawn his attention to her—a flash of some kind? Heat lightning? Whatever it had been, he shouldn't have looked at her. Just one glance strengthened the pull that he always felt in her presence, and immediately his control began to ebb. He glanced down to where her fingers were worrying the hem of her skirt. That was all it took to have him wanting to put his hand right where hers was. No, it was much more than wanting...he *had* to touch her.

He wasn't even aware that he'd moved toward her until his hands were on her shoulders, dragging her to her feet. "I want you."

Then before she could even speak, he took her mouth. Even as her taste poured into him, he felt the blood drain out of his head so quickly, so completely, that he swayed for a moment.

She moved into him, wrapping her arms around him, and her surrender moved through him like a drug. Then his mind went blank and filled with sensations—her tart, sweet taste; the soft press of her body as she moved against him; the hoarse little sound she made in her throat when he nipped at her bottom lip. He moved his hands down her in one possessive stroke, gripping her hips and pulling her higher until they were pressed together, heat to heat. Even when she wrapped her legs around him, it wasn't enough.

He tore his mouth from hers to drag in a breath. The scent of some exotic flower filled his nostrils just as an image filled his mind of taking her on a deserted, moonlit beach while the surf pounded into the shore. He staggered once and then sank onto the bench with her still wrapped around him. He simply had to have her. Right here. Right now.

The first ring of the phone came from far away. The second ring was sharper and penetrated the haze in his brain. For the first time since he'd glanced over at her, a sense of his surroundings flooded into his mind. With breath burning in his lungs, he jerked back. Her face was flushed, her lips swollen, and her eyes...

His mouth was nearly touching hers again when the phone rang a third time.

"We can't," he said, drawing back as her arms tightened around him. "We can't," he repeated, tightening his grip on her and settling her firmly on the bench next to him. His hands trembled as he reached for the phone that lay on the ground. He would have gotten up and moved away from the temptation of touching her again, but he was very much afraid that his legs wouldn't hold him. He settled for easing himself down the bench a little. "What?"

"Jack? We got cut off."

Drawing in a deep breath, Jack tried very hard to concentrate on D.C.'s annoyed voice in his ear.

"About accessing those files. I'll have to send Mrs. Abernathy down to the tombs because they won't be on the computer. It's going to be the same thing at the FBI—if they decide to cooperate."

"Your point being?"

"It's going to take time—perhaps a day or two."

Hawthorne's estimate had only been slightly better for tracking down the person who'd e-mailed Edie.

"At least I don't have to supply you with pizza," Jack said.

D.C. sighed. "I take it you're using Hawthorne. Remember that I rescued that kid from a life of crime."

"You know what? The kid's in need of a good father figure. I think I'll invite him to come out on the boat with us."

"Just as long as you don't tell me what illegal stuff you're having him do for you. In the meantime, I don't like the idea of the two of you poking around out there at the winery until we know a little more. Why don't you just come back to the city and hole up for a while?"

"I'm way ahead of you. I've arranged for Corie to check into Jake Monahan's hotel. He's got first-rate security."

"Good thinking," D.C. said.

"Call me the minute you have anything." As he slipped

the phone back into his pocket, he allowed himself to look at Corie for the first time since he'd moved away from her. She was busily drawing in her notebook again. He wasn't sure what to say. He wasn't in the habit of grabbing women. She was different for him in so many ways that she baffled him. Frustrated, he glanced down at her notebook. It took a moment for the gist of the drawing of the brick wall to register and then he threw back his head and laughed.

Horatio blinked and gave a yip.

Reaching down, Corie patted the dog until his eyes closed again. Then she turned to look at him. "What's so funny?"

Jack lifted the sketch. "This. You ever think of going to art school?"

She smiled. "I think it's safe to say I'd flunk the aptitude test. Doodling helps me think. Usually."

His expression sobered. "Any investigation takes time. And you always run into brick walls." Though he knew it was a mistake, he reached over to tuck a strand of hair behind her ear, and once again she leaned her cheek against his hand.

"This has got to be more than you bargained for when you decided to come out here. Maybe you should let me handle it and go back to Fairview."

"No, I'm not going back." She met his eyes steadily. "I can't do that until I find out exactly what happened to make my mother go into the witness protection program and live in fear all her life. And I'm going to meet Benny. I want to know whether or not he's my father. Even if he doesn't want me, I have a right to know."

"Okay." He could relate to that kind of tenaciousness and admire it. But he also felt relieved that she was sticking around. No, it was more than relief he was feeling. "Going on the theory that your mother saw something she shouldn't have, I've got my assistant at the *Chronicle* checking on all the crimes that were committed in the area during the time just before your mother left town. It's a long shot, but he may turn up something that will help. I've also got him raking through everything he can find on Buddy and Rose. They were both on the boat the day your mom disappeared. He's also checking into any other disappearances of people working for the winery."

Corie closed her hand over his wrist. "You're thinking about your aunt, aren't you? Do you think that she was taken into the witness protection program, too?"

"I don't know what to think." The possibility had been there, pushing at the edges of his mind ever since their conversation with Edie. He'd brushed it aside, not allowing himself to think about it, but he hadn't been quite able to keep his mind from circling back to the possibility— however thin—that his aunt might still be alive. To think, to even talk about it was to hope.... Then suddenly, he found himself telling her about believing he'd seen his Aunt Mel at his college graduation and about the anonymous fan letters. "I'm sure it's all wishful thinking. I keep telling myself that a good investigative reporter has to be objective. And if she was alive all these years, she would have found a way to get in touch with me."

"Unless she thought she would put you in danger if she did. And maybe she did write those letters. That might have been her way of keeping in touch."

There was understanding in her eyes. He didn't know why, but somehow sitting here talking to her felt right— just as it had in the car. "Corie, about what happened a few minutes ago when I kissed you, I'm sorry, I—"

"No, please don't apologize. I've been coming on pretty strong."

"I grabbed *you*."

"Yes, but I told you that I wanted to make love to you this morning. I still do, but I'm not very skilled at this sort of thing."

Skilled? He would have laughed at that if she hadn't had such a serious expression on her face. There was such a straightforward honesty about her. And each time he looked at her he seemed to see more, to wonder how much more there was to see. No other woman had made him want to spend time finding out all there was.

"Reggie and Morgan claimed that just being straightforward and specific always worked for them, and I figured I only had a week in San Francisco. But I've decided I'm not being fair to you. You're helping me, and now there's this possibility about your aunt. I just want you to know that I'm going to back off."

Jack simply stared at her. Just when he thought he was getting a handle on her, she threw something at him he wasn't expecting. Of course, backing off was a good idea for both of them. Logical. They had answers to find. And he had to remember where they were. The clink of glasses and the conversation of diners carried quite clearly on the still air. At their feet, Horatio sighed. On the street beyond the diner, a car backfired.

They both jumped.

In the few seconds that it took for his heart to settle, Jack broke free of his paralysis and raised his other hand to grip her chin. "You're in danger, and we need to find out why. And there are people on the other side of that hedge." He spoke as much for his own benefit as hers. "Rollo is due to check on us at any minute, and Edie will be back, too. Those are three reasons why your back-off plan is good. But there are others. Number one, when we do make love, I want you to be safe. Number two, I intend to take my time."

CORIE HADN'T KNOWN it was possible to melt into a pool of lust just from the way a man looked at you and talked to you. His fingers were barely brushing the back of her ear and his other hand was clasping her chin. They touched nowhere else, and yet she could imagine what it might be like to have him touch every part of her. A shudder moved through her.

When he'd said, "We can't," and pushed her away, she'd almost given into despair. Sidney's back-off-and-tempt plan had been her only option. But now…she didn't want to wait. She didn't think she could.

"Jack…let's not…" She laid her hand on the side of his cheek to draw him closer.

Horatio started to bark. Rising to his feet, he raced toward the tall hedge that bordered Edie's garden, separating it from the road. A second later, she saw something pop up over the top of the hedge. Corie barely had time to register that it was a hat before something shot over the hedge. In the next instant it whipped past her and thwacked into the trellis. Even as Jack shoved her down on the bench, Horatio was barking his head off. Then Jack was rolling her onto the ground.

"Over there. It came over the hedge," she said, trying to make herself heard above Horatio's yapping. She shoved against Jack and experienced exactly what it was really like to push into a brick wall.

"Let me up," she managed on the minimal amount of breath she could drag in. "We might be able to—"

Jack scrambled to his feet before she could finish the sentence and pulled her up. They were both racing toward the hedge when Rollo appeared on the path.

"This way!" Jack shouted.

When they reached the hedge, they couldn't find a break big enough to get through and by the time they reached the end, all they could see was the back of a man wearing a brown hat as he threw himself through the open door of a white van. The next second the van was roaring up the road, spitting out a plume of dust. Horatio barked and chased after it with Rollo in hot pursuit.

"The van had a logo on it," she said. "A *C* intertwined with a *W* and an *S*. I've seen it somewhere…"

"It's the logo for the Crystal Water Spa," Jack said. "That's the one that Benny's sister-in-law Rose runs for the Lewises. It's located right down the road a ways."

"Based on that and the hat he was wearing, plus the fact that Horatio was acting like he knew whoever it was who threw that rock, I'd say it's a pretty safe bet that our 'blind' gunman is connected to the Lewises and wants me to go back to Fairview."

Jack took her hand. "I'm taking you back to San Francisco."

"No."

"Corie—"

She pulled him with her back to the bench. "I just remembered where I saw that logo before." Grabbing her bag, she rummaged through it. "It was on one of the cards the girls gave me at Club Nuevo. Here." She held out Reggie's card. "It's a pass that will get us into the Crystal Water Spa. I bet if we hurry, we might just find the person who tossed that rock just now."

Jack leaned over to pick up the rock and unwrapped the message. The letters had been cut out of the glossy pages of magazines and he read it out loud. "You have something that belongs to me. Bring it to the bar at the Monahan House hotel in San Francisco tomorrow, 5:00 p.m."

"Monahan House," Corie said. "It's a popular place."

"Yes." Jack frowned down at the message. "Benny's party starts with cocktails at six in the ballroom. With most of the bigwigs in San Francisco scheduled to be there, my friend Jake will have his security people all over the hotel. If what they're trying to do is scare you off, why are they practically inviting you to the party? It doesn't make sense."

"Well, it makes just as much sense as everything else that's gone on—blind gunman, arrows, abandoned dogs."

He looked at her then, saw the smile in her eyes and some of his tension eased. "Good point." Then he laid a hand on the side of her cheek. "You're amazing. I'm not sure that if I were in your shoes, I could see the humor in this situation."

"I didn't come out here expecting to find a father who wanted me. I figured if he had, my mother wouldn't have run away to Ohio."

"He was a fool if he didn't want you," Jack said. Then he simply pulled her into his arms and held her. The rush of emotions came, but unlike the other times, he knew what he was feeling. Kinship. Perhaps it wasn't the differences between them that fed his hunger, but the similarities. He'd learned what it was like not to be wanted in the foster home he'd been in before Mel Kincaid had come home and taken him away with her. He'd never have predicted that he would have anything in common with a small-town college librarian, but he could no longer deny that he did. The thought should have scared him. It might have if he hadn't felt so right standing there, just holding her.

She drew back first and raised her eyes to meet his. "What's our next move?"

Perhaps it was the color of her eyes, or perhaps it was

the trust he saw in them that hit him hard. He couldn't be sure, but he felt as if he were sinking again.

"I vote for visiting the Crystal Water Spa," Corie said.

"We are not going to the spa," Jack said, gathering his thoughts quickly. "I'm going to have Rollo take you back to San Francisco. I've made all the arrangements."

Corie stepped back from him then. "Forget it. You just want to hole me up somewhere with Rollo so that you can poke around the spa on your own."

"Corie—"

She held up a hand. "If you go there alone, you're going to stick out like a sore thumb. And if someone recognizes you as Jack Kincaid, you'll be shown the door. Besides, we're partners." She grinned at him as she waved Reggie's business card in front of his nose. "And I have the pass that will get us in." Turning on her heel, she walked to the edge of the arbor before she turned. "Coming?"

"Just remember that you're the junior partner," Jack grumbled as he followed her.

9

CORIE AIMED HER BEST SMILE at the anorexic brunette behind the reception desk. The waiting room at the Crystal Water Spa was large and airy and pink—pink walls, pink chairs, even pink flowers. The effect was enough to make Corie feel a little plain in her white T-shirt and black skirt.

The brunette whose name tag read Lisa was ignoring her and smiling at Jack. Who could blame her? Corie could tell by watching Jack's reflection in the wall of glass behind Lisa that his dimple was operating at full power.

Beyond the glass, a courtyard with a fountain at its center separated the four wings of the building. Each was bordered by a portico and dotted intermittently by windows and doors. A woman swathed from head to toe in towels was being ushered by a pink uniformed attendant through one of the doors. According to the brochure prominently displayed on Lisa's desk, each door led to a room that contained its own private bath and massage area. The Crystal Water Spa promised luxury and privacy.

Step one of the plan she and Jack had hatched on the way over was to get in to see Reggie. After that, they were going to play it by ear. Corie cleared her throat to get Lisa's attention.

"I'll be with you in one minute," Lisa said, not taking her gaze from Jack. "Can I help you, sir?"

It occurred to Corie that a day ago she would have been intimidated, but that was B.L. and B.J. *Before Lorenzo* had transformed her and *before Jack* had told her that he wanted to take his time making love to her.

Whipping out the card Reggie had given her, she passed it to Lisa. "He's with me, and I'd like to see Reggie. I have a complimentary pass."

"So I see." Shifting her gaze to the appointment book, Lisa pursed her lips, then ran a pink-polished fingernail down a page. "Reggie is booked solid today until four."

Corie sighed and glanced beseechingly at Jack. "Can we wait?"

Jack smiled at Lisa, moving to ease a hip onto her desk. "My sister and I were having lunch at the Saratoga Grill and we happened to see one of your vans with the spa logo on it. Since she had the pass, we thought we'd take a chance. She's the impulsive type. Could you check with Reggie and see if he could squeeze her in? Then I could just wait here in the lobby for her. You wouldn't mind if I waited for her, would you?"

"Well," Lisa paused to beam a smile at Jack, "I suppose it wouldn't hurt to check." She picked up her phone and punched in a number.

Jack's dimple should be registered as a lethal weapon, Corie thought. Even reflected in the glass and aimed at someone else, it packed a punch. Lisa couldn't seem to take her eyes off of it.

"Reggie's not picking up. That usually means he's in the middle of a massage. He can't stop without breaking his rhythm."

"Quite understandable," Jack said.

Through the window, Corie saw a man wearing sunglasses and a brown hat step through one of the doors into the courtyard. Meeting Jack's gaze in the glass, she pointed. He leaned a little closer to Lisa. "Would it interrupt Reggie's rhythm if we just went down to his room and asked if he could fit my sister in? He did insist that she should stop by if we were in the area."

"Let me try just one more time," she said as she punched numbers into the phone. "Reggie." She beamed a smile at Jack as she explained their request to Reggie, then she shifted her gaze to Corie. "He says to go right down. It's the third door on the right."

Jack eased his hip off the desk. "I'll just escort her down there and say a quick hello to Reggie. Be right back."

The expression on Lisa's face wasn't happy, but before she could object, Jack was urging Corie through the door into the portico that ran around the courtyard. Corie spotted the man in the brown hat again just skirting the fountain. She nudged Jack with her elbow. They were able to keep him in view until he disappeared through a door at the far end of the courtyard.

Then a door just ahead of them swung open.

"Sugar!"

Corie found herself completely enveloped in Reggie's arms. When he drew back, his grin was wide and welcoming. "You look even better than you did at Club Nuevo."

"So do you," Corie said. And he did. While he made an attractive woman, Reggie was a total knockout as a man. When he ushered them into a room, Jack kept the door open and scanned the courtyard.

"You're beautiful," Corie finally said.

"Look who's talking. Sidney and Morgan can't wait until Saturday night."

"I hate to break up this mutual admiration society," Jack said, "but we're pressed for time and we could use your help."

Reggie's expression sobered. "What's up?"

"It's a long story. The short version is that we followed a man in a white Crystal Water Spa van here after he threw a rock at Corie. We think he's the same man who shot a gun at the airport and later shot an arrow into the apartment building where Corie is staying. We just saw him again. He's medium height, wearing a brown hat and sunglasses."

"You're describing Buddy Lewis. He's been wearing that hat and shades ever since he had his cataracts removed. But he couldn't be your gunman. Buddy wouldn't hurt a fly."

"I'd still like to talk to him," Jack said. "Corie's safety may depend on your helping us."

"What do you want me to do?" Reggie asked.

"Hopefully nothing that will get you in trouble. He just disappeared into a room at the far end of the courtyard." Jack pointed out the spot to Reggie.

"That's Rose's office. He's been here a lot this week, and each time he leaves, Rose is in a foul mood."

"I'd like to talk to him without attracting any attention. Lisa will have her eye peeled on the courtyard. She's expecting me back in the reception area in a few minutes, and I don't think she'll be happy if she sees me walking into Rose's office. She wasn't particularly overjoyed when I brought Corie down here. Do you have a spare uniform I could borrow?"

"Two," Corie said. "I'm going with Jack."

"I only have one spare, sugar," Reggie said as he took it out of a small closet, "and it wouldn't fit you anyway."

"Then I'll wear a towel." She turned to meet Jack's eyes. "I'm going with you."

This time it was the two men who exchanged looks.

"It'll work," Reggie said. "You and I are about the same height, and we have the same coloring. Keep close to the wall, and Lisa will think that I'm taking Corie to Rose for a consultation."

A few moments later, Corie stopped behind Jack at the far side of the portico. Rose's office had a wall of glass just like the reception area. In the quick glimpse that Jack allowed her before he drew her past it, Corie caught sight of a desk and a wall of files. Then Jack opened the door and ushered her through.

The room was empty but roses were everywhere—in the paintings that hung on the walls, in the chintz that covered two sofas, and in vases on the simply styled Swedish furniture. The nameplate on the desk read Rose Morelli. Benny's sister-in-law.

A woman's voice, soft but cold, floated through the opening in a sliding glass door. "I've given you several chances and you've failed me. Your brother's plane is arriving at five this evening. You promised that you would handle the matter before he got back."

"I promise—"

"No. Don't say another word. I'll take care of it myself."

Tightening his grip on Corie's hand, Jack moved closer to the glass door. A tall, stunning woman in a flowing rose-covered caftan sat in a chaise lounge talking to a man wearing a brown hat and sunglasses.

"Rose, you can't—"

The woman rose from the lounge. "Don't you tell me what I can or can't do, not after all the lies you've told me. You've failed me for the last time."

"I did it for you."

"No." She raised a hand to cut him off. "You did it because you're a coward."

Buddy flinched at the word, but Rose continued, "You've always been a coward. That's why your brother moved out here and went into the wine business. And take that hat off. You look ridiculous in it."

"It keeps the sun off," he said as he removed the hat.

If Corie'd had any doubts that the man was Buddy
Lewis, they disappeared the minute Corie saw his face.
Even with sunglasses on, he looked very much like the
photo Jack had shown her, and, once again, the resemblance to Benny was strong. But Buddy looked older, and
his features were softer.

"And don't wear that hat tomorrow night. Your brother
has waited twenty-six years to be recognized by the San
Francisco community. I don't want him to be embarrassed.
Do I make myself clear?"

"Yes, Rose."

She began to pace. "I also don't want him worrying
about that dog. Everything has to run smoothly tomorrow
night. He's going to be worried once you tell him that Horatio is at the vet's. The last thing I want is for Benny to
come back here early after the reception to check on that
foolish dog."

Buddy cleared his throat. "I've arranged for Horatio to
be brought to the hotel before the party tomorrow."

"See that you don't bungle it." She waved a hand in dismissal. "Go. The outside way, not through the spa. Benny
will be home in a couple of hours, and we're dressing for a
family dinner tonight."

As Corie watched Buddy hang his head, then turn and
walk away, she felt a pang of sympathy for him.

"C'mon," Jack said, pulling her back toward the courtyard door. "Maybe we can catch him before he gets to his
car."

They'd taken two steps when the phone on Rose's desk
rang. Turning on his heel, Jack drew her through the door
closest at hand, leaving it open just a crack. They were in a
large storage room. In the dim light filtering through the
frosted glass on the courtyard door, Corie could make out

laundry carts and shelves stacked with pink towels. On the far wall was a cupboard door marked Laundry Chute.

The phone rang again just as Rose reached for it. "Yes?" She sat down in the chair. "Relax. Everything is going according to plan. The shipment is being loaded tomorrow night when everyone is at the dinner. We have nothing to worry about. I would know if he suspected anything."

Rose tapped her fingers impatiently on the desk as she listened to whomever was on the other end of the line. "You'll just have to trust me. I've worked too hard to let anyone or anything interfere with this now. You'll get your shipment on schedule."

There was a pause, then a knock at the door.

"I have to go."

Corie heard the sound of the receiver being replaced, then Rose said, "Come in."

"I'm sorry to disturb you, Ms. Morelli."

"What is it, Lisa?"

"There was a woman who had a complimentary pass from Reggie. He says that he took her to the sauna, but I thought I saw him bring her here."

"As you can see she's not here."

"She's not in the sauna either, and I'm looking for the man who was with her. He was supposed to come back to the reception area, but I can't locate him either."

The moment Lisa began to speak, Jack moved toward the door to the courtyard and opened it a crack. Corie followed him only to have him shake his head and urge her back. Leaning down, he whispered in her ear. "I want to make them think we've left. But before we do, I want to check the caller ID on Rose's phone and find out who that phone call came from."

"And you say she was with her brother?" Rose was asking.

"Yes. Reggie claims he came back to the reception area, but he didn't."

"What did they look like?"

"The man was tall, dark-haired and good-looking. The woman was short with blond hair."

"We need a place to hide." Jack's voice was barely a whisper in Corie's ear as he urged her toward a cupboard marked Laundry Chute and pulled the door open. "Did you like slides when you were a kid?"

She managed a nod. The opening was large and very dark. She could just make out the steep slope of stainless steel. Jack climbed in first, then braced himself, holding onto the edge with one hand. Taking a deep breath, she levered herself up and poked her feet into the pit. He tugged and she wiggled until they were face-to-face, their bodies aligned. With one hand she gripped the edge of the chute.

"Can you close the door?" he whispered.

She did what he asked, and just the small shift had her sliding a little. He slipped his free arm around her.

"Put your arms around my neck," Jack whispered. "Flatten one hand on the wall just as I'm doing. Good."

His face was so close that she could feel his breath fan over her skin.

"Now press your body back against the other wall."

She did, moving carefully because she couldn't see him at all anymore. And perhaps because she couldn't, all of her other senses seemed to be intensified. She could feel him—the hardness of his body where hers brushed against it and the heat at every contact point. Even the rough texture of his linen jacket on the underside of her arms sent a little ribbon of heat through her.

"There's your answer."

Corie stiffened at the sound of Rose's muffled voice.

"They went out through that door to the courtyard," Rose said.

"But why would they have come in your office and not waited to talk to you?" Lisa asked.

"Good question. And I want the answer to it. Why don't you go and see if they're with Reggie? I'll phone security."

Corie counted to ten, then let out the breath she was holding.

"Are you okay?" Jack asked.

"Yes." But that was a lie. She felt totally surrounded by Jack Kincaid. And she wanted to get even closer.

"It won't be much longer. I just want to make sure that the coast is clear."

Just the sound of Jack's whisper, the brush of his breath on her skin, reminded her of the proximity of his mouth. She wanted to kiss him. The back-off-and-tempt plan that she'd opted for in Edie's garden didn't seem important anymore, not when she simply couldn't stop herself.

She leaned forward at the same time that she drew his face toward hers, and at last her mouth brushed against Jack's. The kiss was soft at first. Just the pressure of lips against lips, teasing, nibbling.

"This isn't...a good idea," Jack whispered as he nipped at her bottom lip.

Fighting the weakness that immediately streamed through her, Corie pressed her hand harder against the wall of the chute. Each time Jack Kincaid had touched her or kissed her, the intensity of the pleasure had built, but so had the need. Now desire had turned into so sharp an ache, she wasn't sure she could stand it anymore. Especially, when he was this close. And he couldn't move away. She might never have him at this kind of disadvantage again. Drawing in a deep breath, she pushed one hand more firmly against the wall of the chute, then loosened her grip on Jack's shoulder and let her fingers brush over the damp skin on his neck, then up to his chin.

"Corie..."

"I have the wildest urge to taste you right there," she said, pressing her finger into his dimple.

"What happened to your back-off plan?"

"This is a variation of it." She trailed her fingers down to the neck of his T-shirt and then slowly down his chest.

Jack's laugh sounded muted, strangled. "Really. I think you're going to have to explain that to me."

"Be happy to." She was much better at explanations than at what she was doing. But the quick beat of his heart against the palm of her hand was increasing her confidence. "The theory behind the back-off plan is temptation. Sidney says that men always want what's just out of reach."

"But neither one of us is out of reach."

"No,' Corie agreed, moving her fingers lower, to the waistband of his jeans, and enjoying the shudder that moved through him. "But we really can't do very much or we'll fall down the chute. So what both of us really want is still out of reach."

"Want to bet?" It was self-defense, Jack told himself as he leaned forward to take her mouth. He was doing it to distract her and to save both of them from sliding down the chute into heaven knew what. If either of them moved too much, the fragile traction they'd established to hold themselves in place would fail. Therefore, kissing her was the sane, logical thing to do. But the moment that his lips found hers, he felt his sanity begin to fray. Her mouth was so soft, so silky, so yielding that his head began to swim. He couldn't seem to get enough. He would never be able to get enough. That thought should have given him the strength to pull back. It didn't.

It was only when he felt them both begin to slip that he tore his mouth from hers and pressed his back hard against the wall of the chute.

For a moment, neither one of them spoke. The only sound in the cramped space was the ragged sound of their breathing. Pressing his knee more firmly against the opposite side of the chute, Jack drew his fingertips down her chest, imitating exactly what she'd done to him only moments before.

"Let me see if I've got the back-off plan right," he said as he paused to rub a thumb over the tip of her breast.

His fingers were moving slowly down her stomach, and Corie could feel her body melting inch by inch. All she could hear was the sound of her breathing or was it his? His hand was on her thigh, slipping beneath the skirt and moving up her leg.

"I was thinking about doing this in the car," he whispered. "It nearly made me drive off the road."

She wouldn't have cared, Corie thought. As long as he touched her. *Yes*, she thought as she felt his fingers slide beneath the leg band of her panties.

"Please," she whispered.

"You're driving me crazy," Jack said. And because he simply couldn't help himself, he took her mouth again as he found her heat with his hand.

"This is the last room."

Jack went perfectly still at the sound of the deep, male voice.

"They're not here either," another male voice commented.

"Surprise, surprise," the first man said, his voice even closer now. "If you ask me, La Signora is getting paranoid lately. What is she worried about—that someone is going to steal her beauty secrets?"

"Hey, I'm not complaining. Ever since she beefed up security on the lower level, my salary has doubled."

The other man snorted. "What could be so important about a bunch of bath salts? That's what I'd like to know. Is she afraid that someone is going to steal her formula?"

"Who cares? This is the last room. She's not going to like that we've come up empty."

The other man laughed. "She's gone up to the house. We'll let Hank make the call and give her the bad news. He gets paid to take the heat."

The door slammed and the voices faded. Neither Corie nor Jack moved for several seconds. Then Jack broke the silence. "We're getting out of here. You first."

Corie felt bereft when Jack took his hand away and pressed himself back against the wall of the chute. She was astonished that she could even move her arm when she lifted it to open the door.

"I'll give you a boost," Jack said, placing his hand on her bottom and shoving. Even then it took all her energy and concentration as she pulled and wiggled and muscled herself through the door of the chute. A moment later, he followed her into the storage room.

Even in the dim light making its way through the frosted glass on the door, Jack looked big and dark and...she wanted his hands on her again. She wanted her hands on him.

"Wait here," he said as he moved to the door and pressed his ear against it. "I'm going to check the caller ID."

Of course, he was, Corie thought as he eased the door open and disappeared. She could have wept with frustration. Every single time she tried to seduce this man, he found the strength to walk away, leaving her wallowing in a puddle of lust. Even as she followed him, she thought of how his hand had felt sliding slowly up her thigh and of what might have happened if the security men hadn't interrupted them....

Just thinking about it made her stop and grip the doorjamb for support. She was a mess, but Jack was crouching behind Rose's desk with the phone in his hand, totally focused. As she watched him scribble something on a piece of paper, admiration filled her. Then, still hidden behind the desk, he punched in a number on his cell phone. The man never lost his focus.

"D.C., I've got a number I want you to trace—718-555-3920. Yeah, it's very important. Rose Morelli is doing business with someone in New Jersey."

Maybe Reggie and his friends weren't the only ones she could learn from, she thought. Each time that Jack pulled back from her, she'd withdrawn too, letting her own fears and insecurities stop her. Perhaps, the secret to seducing Jack Kincaid was to remain as focused and determined as he was.

As she listened to Jack give a succinct summary of the rock-throwing incident, Corie straightened away from the doorjamb, moved to the desk and settled her hip up on the corner—just as she had seen Jack do with Lisa.

"One other thing..."

The fact that his sentence trailed off the moment he glanced up and saw her shot her confidence up several notches.

"I told you to wait in the supply room," Jack said.

Corie drew in a deep breath. "I couldn't wait any longer."

"No, not you," Jack said into his phone. "Look..."

His sentence trailed away again as she slipped her fingers beneath the hem of her skirt and inched it up a bit.

"I can't wait even one more minute," she said.

Jack swore as he rose from his crouched position behind the desk. "No, I'm not talking to you, I'm...I...I'll call you back." He stuffed his cell phone into his pocket and when he met her eyes, his were so hot they nearly seared her skin. "Anyone walking by could see you through the windows."

"I'll go back in the supply room if you'll come with me."

"Corie, if I go back in there with you—"

Rising, she began to back toward the supply room door. "We can begin just where we left off in the chute."

"The guards—"

"The guards just checked it. We weren't there, so they won't be back anytime soon." She backed through the doorway and then held her breath. If he didn't follow in the time it took her to count to three...

10

FOLLOWING HER into that storeroom was crazy, irresponsible. And to even consider making love to her there was out of the question. In some far corner of his brain, Jack was vaguely aware of the little lecture he was giving himself, but it didn't seem to stop him from pushing the door shut behind him and shoving the lock into place. Then he moved to where she was standing against the wall.

"I should be able to stop myself." But he couldn't. He'd hoped that getting away from her, putting a door and a wall between them, would have gotten at least some of the blood pumping back into his brain. But it hadn't worked. The whole time he'd been copying down that New Jersey number, he'd been thinking of Corie, of touching her again. When he'd called D.C., his hand had been shaking so badly that he'd nearly dropped the phone.

From that first day at the airport, she'd been eating away at his self-control until... Moving one hand along her shoulder to her throat, he felt the frantic flutter of her pulse. "I'm going to take you, Corie. Right here. Right now."

"Yes," she said just before his mouth covered hers.

FOR A MOMENT, as his taste poured into her, Corie couldn't move. His hands were everywhere, touching, pressing, molding.

"Do you know how long I've wanted to do this?"

His words, the sound of them vibrating against her skin, that clever mouth nibbling at her shoulder had her breath catching, her heart skipping beats. She tried to concentrate so that she could remember each separate thrill. The scrape of his teeth, the wet heat of his tongue. Then later, she could call them up, relive them when she was alone again.

But Jack wasn't giving her time. She couldn't grasp any single sensation before the next wave of pleasure arrowed through her. He was going so fast. Not fast enough.

"Hurry," she said as she struggled to free his shirt. "You have too many clothes."

Even as she said the words, he had her out of her T-shirt and his fingers were working on the skirt. Giving up on his shirt, she pulled open the snap on his pants. But he was quicker, stronger and, seconds later, she was naked, and he was still fully clothed.

"It's not fair," she said.

"No. It's not fair. I've never wanted anyone like this." As if to prove it, he ran his hands up her sides, then down her back. "I can't wait."

"Don't wait." She arched into him. It seemed she'd waited forever to feel the press of those lean, hard hands at her throat, her breasts—not teasing this time, but demanding. "Keep touching me." A hundred little bolts of pleasure shot through her. His lips scorched her throat. His fingers burned her waist. She hadn't known that it was possible for her body to burn and ache and pound so that any moment she might shatter. Closer. She had to get...

When his hands gripped her bottom, she scooted up and wrapped her legs around him.

"Insane," he breathed as he closed his teeth on the lobe of her ear. That's what he was. He'd imagined making love to her with tenderness, with care. He'd wanted to set the scene at the hotel, give her romance. But the need to touch, to taste, to devour was so huge, he couldn't even seem to catch a breath.

"Now."

He wasn't sure if he'd said the word or thought it. Pressing her back against the wall, he held her there as he fumbled with his pants. He had to be inside her. Slipping his fingers into her, he probed her heat.

The catch of her breath, the stunned pleasure that filled her eyes just before she closed them pushed him closer to the edge. It took everything he had to clamp down on his control long enough to remove the foil packet from his wallet and sheath himself.

"Corie." When she opened her eyes, he said, "Look at me. I want to see you when you take me in." Keeping his gaze locked on hers, he pushed into her, then had to clamp down again on his control. She was so hot, so tight, so wet. Even as he drew back slowly and pushed into her again, he felt her draw him in even farther. Then he felt the first convulsion move through her.

"Mine." The word became a drumbeat in his head as he continued to move inside of her, faster and faster. She met him thrust for thrust until there was nothing but the two of them and a world of mindless pleasure. When she convulsed around him for the second time, he let the madness take him.

CORIE DIDN'T REMEMBER the details of how she ended up on Jack's lap on the floor of the supply room. But she knew that she didn't want to move. He was holding her, cradling her really, and she'd never felt so safe in her entire life. Oh, she knew that he might not be thinking of her. In fact, she was pretty sure that he was thinking about Buddy and Benny and Rose. She could almost hear the wheels turning.

But he was holding her, and she wished the moment could go on forever.

"Are you all right?" Jack finally asked.

"I'm wonderful," she said, lifting her head to meet his eyes. "That was—you were...amazing."

He grinned at her. "So were you." Then he brushed her lips with his. "Utterly amazing."

Corie felt her heart melt. And in spite of how amazing they both had been, she knew that if there was only one minute she could tuck away and hold on to, this one was it.

"C'mon," he said, lifting her off his lap and then standing. "We've got to go."

She rose and began to gather up her clothes. "Where to?"

"I'm taking you back to Edie's and Rollo can drive you to Monahan House."

She paused in the middle of zipping up her skirt. Jack was clearly back to business as usual, and she knew exactly what he was planning. "What will you be doing while I'm at Monahan House?"

"This and that," he said absently as he moved back to the door of Rose's office and flipped the lock.

Corie tucked her T-shirt into the skirt. "I'm staying with you."

He turned back. "Corie—"

She met his eyes. "I know you're going to come back here and poke around some more. Rose was talking on the phone about some kind of shipment that *he* doesn't know about. And the shipment's going out tomorrow night when *he'll* be at the reception. I'm thinking *he* has to be Benny, and Rose is up to something behind his back."

Her mind was as sharp as a tack, Jack thought. Why

couldn't he remember that? "The call that Rose got was from a New Jersey area code. I want to find out what she's shipping, and I'll be safer if I don't have to worry about you."

She fisted her hands on her hips. "Nice try. But there's safety in numbers. I can watch your back. I'm betting whatever it is Rose is shipping is in this building because this is her domain. Benny's domain is the winery, so she wouldn't want to risk putting anything there. Plus, the guards said she's beefed up security, especially on the lower level."

"Yeah." She was definitely good.

"Let's check it out before we leave."

Jack sighed. "Corie, it's too dangerous. I'm not going to argue about this."

She lifted her chin. "Good. Because it'll be much safer if we look for whatever it is now than if you take me back to Edie's and then try to sneak back in here."

She was right. It was always futile to argue with logic.

"And right now we know that Rose isn't here. The guards were going to call her up at the main house. She's probably getting ready for the family dinner. So there's no time like the present."

Jack threw up his hands. "Okay. But you'll do what I tell you."

"Absolutely. What do we do first?"

"We're going down that chute," he said and had the pleasure of seeing her eyes widen. "Unless you want to change your mind?"

Corie swallowed, then walked to the cupboard door and opened it.

What a woman. He wanted to hug her, but instead he grabbed her arm. "Before we take the plunge, you need to get in costume."

A few minutes later, she'd changed into one of the neatly pressed pink uniforms on the shelf, and she'd packed her clothes into a pink canvas bag.

"I'll go first," Jack said as he handed her his cell phone. "You wait until I tap on the wall of the chute before you follow. If I don't tap, then it's your job to call Rollo and D.C. Okay?"

Corie nodded. She didn't want to think what might happen if Jack didn't tap on the chute. Not that there was time to worry since he'd already levered himself in. A second later, his head disappeared.

She'd counted to five when the panic hit. She'd made it to ten when she was flipping open the cell phone. Then she heard the faint tapping on the wall of the chute. Clutching the canvas bag to her side, she climbed into the chute and inched her way down. Then, closing her eyes, she let go.

The ride was fast, and her heart had just lodged in her throat when Jack's arms closed around her.

"You're something," he whispered in her ear, and for a moment longer he simply held her. Then he set her on her feet and stepped back.

A quick look around told her that they were in a laundry area. One wall was lined with large commercial washers, another with dryers. Large canvas baskets overflowed with pink towels and more were stacked on a large table in the center of the room. Jack was already moving toward one of the empty baskets. Pushing it toward her, he said, "Get in."

Corie glanced down, then back up at Jack.

"You said you'd do what you're told. This way if we run into anybody, I look like I'm taking dirty towels to the laundry, and if that story doesn't work, no one knows you're in the basket, so you can call for backup."

Jack could have hugged her when she threw her leg over

the side of the basket and climbed in. The woman picked her battles, and he had to admire her for that.

"My Aunt Mel would have liked you," Jack said as he arranged towels over Corie. "You're a woman of your word."

"Well, I don't think my mom would have liked you," she said. "You're exactly the kind of man she warned me to stay away from."

"I would have won her over," Jack said, then grinned when a muffled snort was Corie's only reply.

Opening a door, he eased the laundry basket to a hallway. The corridor was dimly lit. Doors lined the walls on one side, but each one he tried was locked.

When he came to the first turn, he hesitated, listening. Then, flattening his back against the wall, he peered cautiously around the corner. Light spilled from one of the doors at the far end of the hall, and from the sound of it, a poker game was going on. The security guards, he guessed. Beyond the spill of light, he saw a flight of stairs leading upward.

"What's up?" Corie whispered.

Jack lifted a pink towel. "Security guards. I'm going back the other way."

Turning the basket around, he headed in the opposite direction past the laundry room again and around another turn. Once again, he spotted light spilling out from a doorway. Wheeling the basket slowly past, he glanced in and spotted the long counters fitted with tubes and glass vials. A lab. Backing up, he took a more careful look and saw that it was empty.

"I'll be right back," he whispered to Corie. "Stay here." Moving quickly, he entered the room and walked the length of it between two of the counters. Beyond them was a table lined with glass bottles in various sizes. Picking one up, he studied it more closely. It was filled with white powder. The label read Crystal Water Spa Bath Salts.

Bath salts?

"What are you doing in here?"

Jack slipped the bottle into the roomy pocket of his uniform before he turned around to see a tall man in a white lab coat walking toward him. Though his hair was thinning and the wire-rimmed glasses he wore made him look older, Jack guessed his age to be early forties. Smiling at him, Jack held out his hand. "Harry Small."

The man ignored the hand, but said, "I'm Dr. Mazer, and I want to know what you're doing in my lab."

"I was just headed toward the laundry with a load, and I thought I'd see if you had anything."

The man's eyes narrowed, studying him. "No one ever stops by here for laundry. This area of the building is off limits to the rest of the staff."

"My mistake," Jack said easily as he sidled to the other side of the long table. "This is my first week on the job. And I didn't mean to intrude. It's just that the door was open and chemistry was my favorite class in high school." He glanced around the room. "This is a great setup you've got here."

"Right," the man said, pulling a cell phone out of his pocket. "I'm going to have to report this to security."

Jack raised his hands, palms outward, as he edged farther along the table. "Hey. There's no need to report me." He and Mazer were facing each other across an array of vials and rubber tubing. Then he could have cursed himself. Out of the corner of his eye, he saw Corie climb out of the laundry basket and start toward them.

"I'll let them decide that," Mazer said as he flipped open the top of his phone.

"Harry. What in hell are you doing here?" Corie asked, streaking toward them on Mazer's side of the long table.

The Doc whirled to face her and nearly dropped his phone. "Who are—?"

Corie spared him a glance and held up one finger. "In a minute." Then, hands on hips, she sent a withering look at Jack. "I told you to wait for me at the first turn. *First turn,*" she repeated, spacing the words as if she were talking to a very small child. "You have wandered into an off-limits area. That makes both of us look bad." Then she pointed her finger at the door. "Go. Wait for me in the hall."

Jack went, not because he liked it, but because he could see that Corie's little act was working. Dr. Mazer wasn't punching numbers into his cell phone.

"I am soooo sorry about that," Corie said, her tone changing from vinegar to sugar. "I have no excuse except that he's new on the job." Then in a hushed voice, she continued. "And he's a little slow."

"Slow?" Mazer asked.

Turning in the doorway, Jack saw her signal Mazer to lean a little closer. "You know. His pilot light isn't on all the time." Now her voice was low, breathy and sexy as hell.

"But he has the most wonderful hands, and he's getting to be very popular with the clientele," Corie continued.

"Oh," Mazer said.

"I'm surprised that he could even tell this was a lab." She glanced around. "It's beautiful. You must be very smart."

"Well, I—"

"I would really appreciate it a lot if you didn't report this," Corie said, running one finger down the buttons of his lab coat. "I could get in trouble since Harry's my responsibility. And I'll make sure he doesn't do this again."

Mazer cleared his throat. "Well, if you'll make sure it doesn't happen again—"

"Thank you soooo much," Corie said, backing toward the door. "If you want a really great massage that will get all the kinks out, you be sure and ask for Sally."

The moment she was out in the corridor, she pushed the door shut and pulled her pink bag out of the laundry basket. "Let's make tracks."

Jack grabbed her arm and drew her toward the staircase at the end of the hall.

"Nice work, Sally," he said as they took the stairs two at a time.

"Thanks," she said, beaming a smile at him. "I did save your butt."

"That you did. And Harry's pilot light was working a little better than either you or the Doc gave him credit for."

She turned to him then, her eyes glowing. "You got something."

He waited until they'd reached the top of the stairs before he took out the bottle he'd hidden in his pocket.

"Bath salts?" Corie asked.

"Maybe, but maybe not. Why would Dr. Mazer and Rose be so concerned with security if all he's making is bath salts?"

Corie glanced at the glass bottle and then back at Jack. "Good question. And Rose seems to be very concerned that Benny not find out about whatever it is she's shipping out tomorrow night."

"And she has a partner in New Jersey." Jack pushed open the door and they stepped out into a parking lot. A quick glance around told him that it wasn't the one they'd parked in. He'd no sooner stepped forward to get a feel for his surroundings when a car squealed across the pavement and stopped in front of them.

When the door swung open, Reggie said, "There's a car in the visitor's lot that has a security guard leaning against its hood. A silver convertible with the top down? I'm assuming that's yours?"

"Yeah," Jack said. And that meant they'd traced the license plates. They'd be watching for him.

"Well, get in," Reggie said. "And tell me where you want to go."

11

Mrs. H,

News update! As I'm writing this, I am sitting in the penthouse suite of one of San Francisco's most exclusive hotels, Monahan House, with the owner, Jake Monahan, and his wife, Torrie! And *yes*, she's that very same Torrie I told you about earlier—the one who originally bought our little man-magnet skirt on that island. Turns out her husband is Jake Monahan, an old friend of Jack's. I was trying to get in touch with her, and now—voilà! I'm here in her living room. I can't wait to interview her and add her story to my collection.

But that will have to wait. Right now, my current screenplay needs my full attention. The plot is thickening at a very rapid pace. Jack and Corie have spent the day in the Napa Valley tracing the identity of the "blind" hit man. And Jack—my hero—has called us all here for an important meeting tonight. "Us" includes Hawthorne, a computer geek; D.C., a police captain who's also an old friend of Jack's; moi, of course. And I brought along Darcy, the young girl I take care of when her mother is out of town. Jack thinks the hotel is a safer place to rendezvous than my apartment building since someone shot an arrow at it last night! I agree.

Wait! Jack and Corie have arrived. To be continued...

FROM THE MOMENT that Corie had entered Jake Monahan's suite on the top floor of his hotel, she'd felt at home. Jake had greeted them at the door and ushered them into a huge living area with a sunken game room and a designer kitchen blocked off by counters at one end. Jake's wife, Torrie, a very pregnant brunette and the executive chef of his hotel, had been shoveling pizza in and out of the ovens when they'd arrived. Franco, Hawthorne, Darcy and D.C. were already seated on cushions around a large coffee table.

"Try the Hawaiian one," Jake had suggested when he handed Corie a glass of wine. "It's my wife's specialty."

Corie hadn't realized how hungry she was until she'd bitten into her first slice. In addition to the pizzas, Torrie had served platters of antipasto. The food had been enough to serve an army, and judging by the number of pizza crusts now littering the plates on the coffee table, they'd eaten like one.

For the past fifteen minutes, Jack had been telling everyone about their little adventure at the Crystal Water Spa.

"And then she says, 'Harry's pilot light isn't always on.'"

"Great line," Franco said, whipping out his notebook.

"After that, she points at the door and orders me to wait in the hall," Jack continued.

"This sounds like a scene from one of those 'buddy' movies," Darcy said.

"You're right," Franco said staring at her across the table. "You're brilliant! *My Fair Lady* meets *Lethal Weapon*. My agent will love that concept."

"If you'd been arrested for B and E, the 'concept' might not have played so well in front of a judge," D.C. pointed out.

"Good thing you're here as a concerned friend, not a cop," Jack said.

"A good defense attorney could make an argument that it wasn't technically B and E," Jake said. "Corie and Jack were clients of the spa, and the lab door *was* left open."

As the men continued to debate the issue, Torrie leaned close to Corie. "I never would have had the courage to go in there and act like that."

Corie smiled. "A week ago, neither would I. Back in my hometown, I have a history of acting on impulse, and I've spent my life trying to control it. But since I've come to San Francisco and met Jack, I'm beginning to think that sometimes going with my impulses is a good thing."

"Yes." Torrie smiled at her. "I sort of decided the same thing when I first met Jake."

D.C. raised both hands in surrender. "All right. All right. Maybe it wasn't strictly speaking breaking and entering. But it was a dangerous thing to do."

"Worth it, though," Jack said as he pulled the bottle of bath salts out of his pocket. "Look what I got."

"Bath salts?" D.C. asked as he read the label. "Where did you get them?"

"Dr. Mazer's secret lab, and I'm betting it's something else," Jack said. "Perhaps designer drugs. That would explain the heightened security at the spa. Plus, the lab is small, and they're not set up to mass-produce anything."

"That's all speculation," D.C. said.

"Rose Morelli is making a shipment to whoever is listed at that number I gave you in New Jersey," Jack pointed out. "That's a fact. And it's scheduled for loading tomorrow night when everyone's attention will be focused on the reception honoring Benny."

D.C. frowned. "It'll take me forever to get this stuff run through the lab downtown."

"I have a contact at a private lab," Jake said rising. "I'll give him a call."

D.C. shook his head and sighed. "It's still a long shot. So far, everything that I've turned up on that phone number you gave me is legit."

Jack stared at him. "You're sure?"

"The company the phone's listed to is New Ventures Communications. It's a small company owned by Carlo and Sally Ventura. I checked with a friend on the Trenton police force, and the Venturas are legit—no connections to any mob family," D.C. said. "They make product videos, buy TV time and provide storage for products in a warehouse they own."

"If the bath salts are just bath salts, then why all the secrecy?" Corie asked.

"Rose Morelli would be the one to ask," D.C. said. "But unless Jake's friend comes up with something in that bottle besides bath salts, I don't have any reason to go poking around at the Crystal Water Spa. And neither do either of you," he said pointedly.

"Then we'll just have to come at it from a different angle," Jack said. "We know that Buddy is our ineffective hit man. From the little scene that Corie and I saw, he might be taking his orders from Rose."

"But we don't know for sure that Rose and Buddy were talking about his attempts to scare me off," Corie said. "She just accused him of lying to her and of being a failure. And what does whatever is going on at the spa have to do with their wanting me to go back to Fairview?"

"They might not be connected at all," D.C. said.

"But I have a feeling they are," Jack said.

The ringing of the phone had Jake reaching for an extension on a nearby table. "Yes?" Covering the mouthpiece, he glanced over at Jack. "Benny Lewis is in the lobby, and he's asking to see you."

Corie felt her stomach muscles clench as Jack met her eyes.

"I'll meet with him down in the lobby," he said.

Corie drew in a deep breath. "No, ask him to come up."

He took her hands. "Are you sure you're ready?"

She wasn't sure she'd ever be ready. But she wasn't going to run away. "Maybe he can answer some of our questions."

Jack nodded before he reached for the phone.

CORIE STOOD UP when Jack ushered Benny Lewis into the suite. Jake and Torrie had ushered Franco and the kids and Horatio into an adjoining room, and D.C. had gone with them. Jack was standing nearby, but she didn't look at him. She couldn't take her eyes off of Benny as he walked across the room toward her.

He was medium height, and his hair was that kind of silver gray that only enhanced his good looks. Charm, charisma, power—she wasn't sure she had a name for what seemed to emanate from the man, but she felt drawn to him at the same time that she wanted very badly to run. When he stopped a short distance away, she braced herself.

"Mr. Kincaid," he said as he nodded at Jack. Then his gaze shifted to Corie. "And you're—" His eyes narrowed as his voice trailed off.

"Corie Benjamin," she said, extending her hand.

When Benny didn't reach for it and merely continued to study her, the small rejection moved through her and she braced herself for more.

"You were Mr. Kincaid's accomplice when he broke into

Dr. Mazer's lab at my spa? The security camera caught your face as you walked out of the lab. It didn't do justice to your eyes."

"Actually, Jack didn't break into the lab," Corie said. "The door was wide open, the room was unattended and he just wandered in. We both did."

Benny waved a hand, dismissing her explanation. "I saw the security tapes, and I recognized Mr. Kincaid immediately. I was present when Dr. Mazer came up to the house in person to tell my sister-in-law. The fact that you were wearing uniforms and impersonating employees undercuts the credibility of your story, and I doubt the police would buy it."

"I...well..." The man had the most piercing eyes. Corie had the distinct feeling that he would see through any lie she tried to make up.

"If you know all that, why didn't you call the police and have us arrested?" Jack asked.

Benny kept his eyes on Corie's. "Because when I saw the tapes, I thought..." For the first moment since he'd walked into the room, Corie saw uncertainty in Benny Lewis's eyes. Then just as quickly as it had appeared, it vanished. "I want to know who you are. I've only seen eyes your color once, Miss...what did you say your name was?"

"Corie Benjamin," she said.

"You remind me of someone."

Corie glanced at Jack, then she drew in a deep breath and said, "The Corie is short for Corinna. I probably remind you of my mother. You knew her as Isabella Corinna. But the name that appears on my birth certificate is Isabella Benjamin, and that's the name she went by in Fairview, Ohio."

Benny's eyes narrowed then and became hard. "Then

the stories were true. She was pregnant, and she ran away with her lover."

"I don't think so," Corie said. "I can't be sure, of course. But I can't remember a time when my mother had anyone in her life, except me. She never dated, and I'm pretty sure you were the only man she ever loved."

Benny raised a hand. "No. You're proof that she loved another."

"I have letters she never sent, and they were all addressed to you. I don't believe that she ever stopped loving you."

"She told you I was your father?" Benny asked, his eyes hard.

"No. She would never talk about my father."

Benny snorted. "If you've come here for money—"

"I don't want your money," Corie said, taking a step toward him. "I came out here to San Francisco to find out if you were my father and to find out why my mother was so afraid of you that she couldn't go out of the house. I'm not going to end up like that."

"Isabella was never afraid of me." Benny stepped forward, closing the small distance between them.

The heat she'd glimpsed in his eyes before was nothing to the ice she saw now. Lifting her chin, she met his eyes squarely. "She lived her whole life afraid of something. I think she ran away from you to protect me, and I want to know why she felt she had to do that."

"I never did anything to make Isabella afraid. You're lying. If you're after money, that's not a good strategy."

"This isn't about money," Jack broke in, the anger clear in his voice. "Corie's your daughter. I can show you the evidence I've gathered, and there are DNA tests that you can run. But all that will take time."

Once again, Benny waved a hand in dismissal. "You'll

hear from my lawyers." Then he turned and moved toward the door.

"Perhaps the most compelling evidence that she's related to you is that someone in your family has been taking shots at her since the day she arrived in San Francisco. When we went to the spa today, we followed your brother, Buddy, after he threw a rock at Corie. And we think he fired a shot at the airport the day she arrived."

Benny whirled toward them then, his eyes so hot that Corie very nearly took a step back. Then he shifted his gaze to Jack, and his voice was very low when he spoke. "Be very careful of what you say about my family. You were quick to judge me once before with no proof."

"We have some proof," Corie said.

"What?" Benny asked.

"When I arrived on Wednesday, a man wearing a hat and sunglasses with a white cane and a dog fired a shot just as we were leaving the airport," she said. "We figured the blind-man getup was a disguise when the dog turned out to be a shih tzu."

"A shih tzu," Benny said.

"Exactly. It's a wonderful breed, but they are not Seeing Eye dogs. Later that night, when someone shot an arrow at the building where I was staying, he left his dog behind."

Benny frowned down at her. "You said you had proof, and all you can come up with is a blind man, arrows and a shih tzu?"

"The two of you are a lot alike," Jack said to Benny. "You're as tough a sell as she is. The shih tzu's name is Horatio," Jack said, moving toward the door to the bedroom. As soon as he opened the door, Horatio raced toward Corie. The minute she scooped him up, the dog spotted Benny and began to wiggle and bark.

"I think he's missed you," she said as she handed the dog to Benny.

"How did you get—?" Benny cut himself off. "Wait." Tucking Horatio under his arm, he reached for Corie's hand and turned it over to study her wrist. "That mark on your wrist..." He raised his eyes to meet Corie's. "How did you get it?"

"It's a birthmark. My mother always told me it marked my heritage."

Benny stared at her for a long minute. "My mother had the same mark and so did my grandmother. You wouldn't have it unless—"

Releasing her wrist, he continued to stare at her. Then he slowly raised his hand to cup the side of her head. "You are my daughter."

Corie raised her hand to cover his as the rush of emotions filled her and the wonder moved through her. He'd said the word *daughter* as if he were trying it out, testing it. She knew exactly how he felt. This was her father. Her *father*. She couldn't quite grasp the reality of it yet.

"I don't understand," Benny finally said. "Where is Isabella? I want to talk to her."

Corie tightened her grip on his hand. He didn't know. "She died two months ago. It was very sudden."

"I'm sorry," he said and drew her closer until her head was pressed against his chest. "I'm so sorry." After a moment, he spoke again, "Why did Isabella run away? Did she think I would be upset because she was pregnant? We'd talked about having children. That was something we both wanted. What was she afraid of?"

"I don't know." Drawing back, Corie saw some of what he was feeling in his eyes—confusion, anger and pain.

"I would never have hurt her," Benny said. "Never."

Corie could see that he was speaking the truth. The need

to comfort was so strong that she linked her fingers with his and drew him toward one of the sofas. "Maybe you can help us find out what scared her. Why don't you sit down?"

Jack moved toward a cabinet and poured brandy into three glasses. It wasn't until a few drops spilled out of the decanter that he realized his hand was shaking. He felt helpless—and furious. *If* Benny were speaking the truth, then someone else was responsible for Isabella's disappearance all those years ago. And that someone had stolen years of love and happiness from Benny and Isabella, and Corie, too.

"Here," he said as he passed out the drinks. They could all use a drink, he thought as he took a long swallow of his own. If he'd had any doubts that Corie was indeed Benny's daughter, they'd vanished the moment she'd strode toward him and faced him toe to toe. That, even more than the birthmark, had been telling. She might be worried that she was like her mother, but that streak of courage was something she'd inherited from her father.

He studied them as they sat together on the sofa. Horatio had settled himself on Corie's lap, and Benny was holding her hand, looking at her as if he was trying to absorb twenty-five years as they talked.

"A college librarian, huh? My mother would have liked that. She always wanted me to go to college. What about your mother?"

"She was an excellent seamstress. She had a real talent for design, and it was the kind of work that allowed her to stay at home."

Benny nodded. "She was always shy."

"I wasn't like her. I always wanted to leave. I always dreamed of traveling."

Benny smiled at her. "I know the feeling. My family

teases me about my wander lust all the time. This past year I bought two vineyards in Italy, so now I have an excuse to travel."

Jack cleared his throat, and Benny glanced at him. "I know that the two of you have a lot to catch up on, but we have to talk about what's going on now."

"Yes," Benny replied. "Perhaps you could explain again how the two of you got hold of my dog?"

"Corie already told you," Jack said. "It's not going to sound any more sensible the second time around."

"Humor me," Benny said.

"A man hid out across the street from my apartment building and when we arrived, he shot an arrow at the house with a note attached, warning Corie to go back to Fairview. Somehow the dog got away from him and ended up under the porch of my apartment building. Corie's been taking care of Horatio ever since. Buddy and Rose didn't mention that Horatio's been missing, I take it?" Jack asked.

"Buddy told me he was at the vet's."

"We think Buddy's been trying to scare Corie away ever since she stepped off the plane," Jack said. "We believe that he's the one who's been disguising himself as a blind man."

"How did he know that she was coming to San Francisco?" Benny paused, and his frown deepened. "How could he possibly even know who she was?"

"Good question," Corie said.

Benny turned to Jack. "How did *you* find out about her?"

Jack briefly summarized all the information they had so far including what they knew and didn't know about his anonymous informant. "We're still trying to trace the identity of the person who sent the e-mails to Edie Brannigan."

"None of it makes sense. The witness protection program? Why on earth would she have been placed in that?"

"I think it's obvious that Buddy knows at least some of the answers," Corie said.

Benny turned to her. "He wouldn't hurt you. He doesn't have the stomach for violence. That's one of the reasons I decided to move out here.... Well, that's another story. My brother could never harm a flea."

"Perhaps not physically. But someone frightened Isabella enough to bury herself in Ohio all those years ago. And someone—Buddy—is trying to do the same thing to Corie now."

Benny's eyes narrowed and his back stiffened. "You're insinuating that my brother had something to do with Isabella's disappearance twenty-five years ago?"

Jack raised both hands, palms out. "All I'm saying is that there's a good chance he knows what happened, and all Corie and I want to do is find out the truth. And, of course, keep her safe. We could use your help."

Instead of answering Jack's question, Benny turned to Corie. "You know that this young man thinks I had something to so with his aunt's disappearance?"

"Yes, but—"

Benny cut her off with a raised hand. "Do you think that I had something to do with it?"

"I don't know you that well." When Benny opened his mouth, it was her turn to hold up a hand. "But I don't think you had anything to do with frightening my mother away. And I have a strong feeling that whoever sent my mother away also had something to do with Mel Kincaid's disappearance. You never really believed Jack, but his aunt called him shortly before she disappeared and said that she'd discovered something at the vineyard, something she was going to check into. What if she'd found out something about my mother's disappearance?"

Benny turned to Jack. "It's a good question."

"She's got a real talent for asking the good ones," Jack said.

Benny studied him for a moment. "How do we go about finding the answer?"

Jack tried not to let the relief he was feeling show on his face. "I'll let you talk to my friend, Jake Monahan. He owns the hotel, and his security is first-rate. Corie is going to meet Buddy in the lounge tomorrow at five. Jake will explain what we have planned. But first, I need your word that you'll let us go ahead with it, and that you won't do anything that will warn Buddy or Rose."

Benny studied Jack, and for a long minute said nothing. Finally, he spoke. "I'll give you my word. I owe you that much for bringing my daughter to me. But you'd better deliver some proof."

"IT'S NOT THAT they're trying to be rude," Torrie Monahan said as she began to gather up the debris from their pizza party. "It's just that boys have their toys. Jake wants to show off all the new security upgrades he's made since he bought this hotel. And men don't think that women can appreciate the intricacies of all the techno mumbo jumbo."

"Are *all* men like that?" Darcy asked. "I thought it was just Hawthorne."

"It's a conspiracy," Corie said, frowning as she scraped a few remains off an antipasto platter and loaded it onto a dumbwaiter. After Jake had explained the setup for her meeting with Buddy in the bar, he'd invited Benny to take a look at his security room, and the women had not been invited. Corie had a hunch she knew why. "Jack just wants a chance to grill Benny when I'm not around."

"And your father probably wants a chance to grill Jack," Torrie said. "It can't be easy to meet a daughter you've never known *and* a man who is in love with her all in one fell swoop."

Corie nearly dropped the plate she was holding. "Jack is not in love with me."

Torrie grinned at her. "If he hasn't taken the tumble yet, he's close. He's got that look on his face like he's in real deep whenever he looks at you. It's kind of like the one you've got when you look at him. And Benny Lewis strikes me as a smart man. If I can see it, I'm sure he sees it too."

"It's not like that," Corie said. "We've just been thrown together because of this mess. He wants to protect me and..."

"That's kind of how Jake and I got together," Torrie said. "I needed his help. We met right in the bar of this hotel."

"Really?" Darcy asked.

Torrie smiled at the memory. "I tried to pick him up."

"Looks like you succeeded," Corie said.

"What's your secret?" Darcy asked, setting the glasses she'd collected on the counter. "I can't seem to get Hawthorne to glance up from his computer screen."

"Well," Torrie said. "It just so happens that I had a little help from a special skirt."

"A skirt?" Corie asked.

"I know it's hard to believe, but in college I went on a cruise with my aunt during spring break and we got blown off course to this island. I picked up this skirt that has a special effect on men."

Corie stared at her. "I think I've got that skirt. Wait, I'll show you." Moving to the door where she'd dropped the pink canvas bag, she unpacked the skirt and shook it out.

Torrie walked over to examine it more closely. "That could be it, I suppose. Although I can't imagine how you got it."

"She got it from Franco," Darcy said. "He rents his apartment to women on a time-share basis and he lends the skirt to them. He's writing a screenplay about their adventures. That's why he's always scribbling those notes."

Torrie rubbed the hem of the skirt between her fingers. "Where did Franco find this skirt?"

"In New York," Darcy explained. "He used to be a doorman at a place there."

Torrie glanced from Darcy to Corie. "The last I heard the skirt *was* in New York. One of my roommates from college sent it to a friend, so this could be the one. Jake will know for sure. Part of the effect it has on men is that they see things in it that women don't."

Darcy ran her hand over the skirt. "That's not fair."

"Well, the upside is that when a woman wears it, the skirt has the power to bring her true love to her," Torrie said.

Corie stared at the skirt. "Franco told me that the skirt attracted men. But he left the part out about how it was supposed to bring me my true love."

"Can I borrow it?" Darcy asked.

"I think you're a little too young to be attracting your true love," Torrie said. "This skirt really has serious powers."

Corie glanced up from the skirt, her mind still spinning. She'd been so sure that she'd changed since she'd come to San Francisco. Was it only because she'd been wearing the skirt? Worse still, was Jack only attracted to her because of some magic spell? For the first time, the realization bloomed inside of her that she didn't want him to be attracted to her only because of the skirt. "I think Torrie's right. This skirt can get you into serious trouble." Then she managed a smile for Darcy. "But if your mother will agree, you could start with a makeover at Lorenzo's. Franco can make the appointment."

"Neat," Darcy said.

JACK RACKED THE BALLS and faced Hawthorne across the pool table. Benny Lewis had finally left, and everyone else had given up and gone to bed.

"I'll spot you two balls this time," Hawthorne said.

"Thanks, kid." Leaning over the table, Jack took careful aim and sent the balls clattering across the table. Hawthorne was good, thanks to the fact that he'd probably spent a lot of lonely hours working on his game. Jack was going to have a little heart-to-heart talk with Hawthorne's dad.

After lining up the next ball, Jack sent it into the corner pocket.

"Nice shot," Hawthorne said.

And an easy one, Jack thought as he took another look at the patterns the balls made on the table. He was off his game tonight. Usually playing pool helped him to relax and think. He'd gone over every single step of the scenario Jake and D.C. had worked up for Corie's meeting with Buddy Lewis tomorrow, and he couldn't see any weaknesses. She was going to wear a wire and try to get him to talk.

Even her father had seemed satisfied with the plan. Jake would have security people stationed at every step of the way—from the time she entered the lobby to when she moved into the bar. And Rollo would be close by. So why was he so uneasy?

"Corie's dad is sure concerned about her," Hawthorne said. "He asked Jake some really good questions."

"Yeah," Jack said. The older man *had* asked a lot of questions, including some probing ones about Jack's relationship with Corie. He'd been able to answer some of them—but he didn't really know how Corie felt.

Already he could feel her slipping away. Whatever happened tomorrow, he had to face the fact that she was going to have a new family. When Benny had hugged her before he'd left, Jack had tasted the bitter, coppery taste of jealousy.

Leaning over the table, he lined up his next shot. All he had to do was nick the cue ball at the right angle and send the seven ball into the pocket. He took the shot, and watched the seven ball move back to the center of the table.

Hawthorne looked at him suspiciously. "Did you do that on purpose?"

Jack smiled ruefully at him. "Relax, kid. You're getting my best game tonight."

Hawthorne held his gaze for another minute, but then shrugged and nodded. "Girls. They mess up your game every time."

"Yeah," Jack said. Hawthorne had it right. He was having trouble thinking straight because he couldn't seem to keep Corie out of his mind for more than a few seconds. It was the wrong time to push her, to ask her if he was anything but a fling to her. She had a role to play tomorrow. For her own safety, she had to be able to give her full attention to that.

He watched Hawthorne sink three fast balls. "Girls don't seem to be messing up your game any."

Hawthorne glanced up, and Jack could have sworn he

was blushing. "Darcy isn't interested in me. She just likes the things I've been teaching her on the computer."

Jack's eyes narrowed. "Just what have you been teaching her?"

"Nothing illegal. Really."

Jack relaxed a little. "Then I think you've got it wrong about Darcy."

"Really?"

"I don't think she's hanging around you for the pizza, kid."

"Oh."

Leaning back against the wall, Jack watched Hawthorne nearly miss his next shot. But then the boy rallied and began to methodically clear the table. Jack wished he could fix his girl problem just as easily.

The whole day was still spinning through his mind. The madness of making love to her in that supply room. He sure as hell hadn't been thinking then. He simply hadn't been able to stop himself.

That scared him. Corie scared him. The truth was he wouldn't push her for answers tonight because he was afraid of what she might say. He'd never let any woman have that kind of power over him before. He'd never needed a woman before the way he needed Corie right now.

"You up for another game?" Hawthorne asked.

"Sure."

Hawthorne racked the balls, "I'll spot you three balls this time."

Jack thought that he might need them as he leaned over to take his first shot. The balls clattered across the table.

"So when you get this all settled tomorrow, where will you be off to?" Hawthorne asked as Jack sent a ball into the pocket.

"Hard to say," Jack said, trying to focus on the game. "My book editor has been begging me to go to the Middle East for some time now."

"The Middle East? That's dangerous," Hawthorne said, the awe clear in his voice.

"I suppose," Jack said. He had the cue ball lined up perfectly when it struck him. He hadn't thought of finishing his book on organized crime in the twenty-first century and flying off to the Middle East since Corie Benjamin had stepped off that plane. The realization struck him that he didn't want to go to the Middle East or anywhere that would take him away from...

The cue ball ricocheted off the side of the table, then shot like an arrow into the corner pocket.

Hell, he couldn't even shoot a decent game of pool anymore. Corie Benjamin was affecting everything in his life.

IN THE HALLWAY, Corie turned and made her way back to the bedroom that Torrie had escorted her to earlier. After letting herself in, she walked toward the windows that filled one wall. Three quick flashes of lightning spiked the sky, and for a second she saw the Golden Gate Bridge in the distance. When the thunder rumbled, Horatio stirred on a nearby chair, then opened his eyes and blinked at her. Earlier, when she'd laid the skirt over the back of the chair, he'd jumped right up, snuggled his head against it and dropped off into doggy dreamland.

She had a feeling sleep was a long way off for her. Jack would be going to the Middle East when this was over. When he'd said that to Hawthorne, a cold numbness had spread through her. She didn't want him to go any more than she wanted to go back to Ohio.

Horatio gave a dreamy little sigh.

"I've made a mess of it, pal," she said.

Horatio sighed again and snuggled more firmly into the skirt. Figures, she thought. And it was about time she faced the fact that Jack Kincaid was a victim of the skirt, too. She thought about what had happened in Edie's garden. She'd been fingering the skirt when he'd grabbed her. And later, in Rose's office, she recalled how she'd pulled the skirt higher on her thigh.

Lightning spiked the sky again, and this time the rumble of thunder was closer.

Horatio gave a soft yip.

"Jack's going away to the Middle East," she said. She had to face reality. But saying it out loud only tightened the band of pain that had clamped itself on her heart the moment she'd overheard him say it.

"And as soon as we find out why Buddy has been shooting bullets, arrows and rocks at me, I'll be going back to Ohio."

Horatio blinked once and then shut his eyes.

That had been her plan, hadn't it? Go to San Francisco, meet her father and figure out why he'd never wanted to see her or her mother again, perhaps have a wild affair with a man—and then retreat back into her existence as a college librarian. For the life of her she couldn't put a finger on the moment when she'd decided to change it. When was it that she had started wanting more?

Perhaps it was when Jack had pinned her against that wall in the supply room. Or maybe it was when he'd just held her in the garden at Edie's. Or maybe it had happened when she'd been in the fitting room at Macy's and she'd looked into the mirror and met Jack's eyes. Something had definitely happened then.

No, she thought suddenly. It wasn't just that her goal had changed. *She'd* changed. She wasn't that pathetic woman who'd wanted to cringe under the table in her mother's house. And it was more than her hair or the new clothes—or even a man-magnet skirt. She'd changed inside, too. She wasn't like her mother. She wasn't afraid to want more. Because she'd fallen in love with Jack Kincaid.

Slowly, she sank down onto the edge of the bed and pressed a hand against her heart. Beneath the swirl of emotions—panic, fear—she felt a steady, quiet joy. She glanced over at Horatio who was sleeping again.

Maybe the skirt had helped a little, and maybe Jack had been affected by it. Worst-case scenario, she'd just have to seduce him again without the skirt.

"Corie..."

Glancing up, she saw her best-case scenario standing in the doorway. He was barefoot, wearing nothing but his jeans and looking incredibly sexy. Temptation personified.

"I shouldn't have come," he said.

"You saved me a trip," she said. It was too late to put on the skirt. *You're the new Corie,* she reminded herself as she willed her feet to carry her across the room. *You don't need a man-magnet skirt.* The moment she saw the mix of confusion and desire in Jack's eyes, she began to believe it.

"We should talk..."

"Shhh." She pressed her fingers against his lips. "No talking. I just want to make love to you." In the back of her mind, she tried to dredge up everything that the "girls" at the Club Nuevo had told her. "But first I want to touch you."

When he reached to pull her closer, she took his hand, raised it to her lips and kissed the palm.

"Not yet," she said as she drew him toward the bed. "You had your wicked way with me in the supply room. Now it's my turn."

Keeping her eyes on his, she ran her hand slowly down his chest. His skin was warm. How could it be so smooth when the muscles beneath were so hard? "I've never really touched a man before. Not like this. I can feel your heartbeat."

When she felt him shiver, delight streamed through her and she moved her hand lower to the waist of his jeans and pulled the snap. His quick intake of air sent a thrill through her, and the look in his eyes told her that he felt it too. Slowly, keeping her eyes on his, she drew down the zipper.

She saw the instant flare of desire in his eyes. Even as the heat of it shot through her, he moved one hand into her hair and the other gripped her hip. And suddenly the edge of the bed was pressing into the back of her legs.

"I want you, Corie."

HIS VOICE sounded breathless, even to his own ears, and he knew she could be beneath him on that mattress in an instant. It was what he wanted, what they both wanted.

Even as the image burned through his brain, she raised her hand to his chest. "Not yet. Fair is fair. This is my turn."

When she urged him to lie on the bed, he complied. Then she climbed up beside him and straddled him. Jack drew in a quick breath. The press of her, the heat of her against his erection had him reaching for her. But she gripped his hands and pressed them into the pillow above his head.

"You're playing with fire," he said.

"When I was a little girl, I was always tempted to strike matches—even though I knew they were forbidden. That bright burst of flame always tempted me."

With her eyes steady on his, she lowered her mouth to his and whispered, "You fascinate me. I want to taste you. All of you." She kissed him slowly, teasing his lips with hers, then went on to explore the line of his jaw, his throat. When she finally returned to his mouth, she didn't linger. He only caught a brief taste of her before she moved on.

Then she began a slow, torturous exploration of his body with her mouth. Inch by inch, he felt his skin dampen and then burn as she tasted him from shoulder to waist. Even as his heart began to thunder in his own ears, weakness seeped through him. When she released his hands, he didn't have the strength to use them. His breath backed up in his lungs when she began to drag his jeans down his legs. He'd felt desire before, from a slow burn to a sizzling fire. But this was different. Corie was different. When her hand closed around his erection, he felt flames sear through him right to his core. Opening his eyes, he saw her rip open the foil packet and begin to sheath him with the condom. Pleasure mixed with pain, and need sharpened to an ache. He began to tremble. His mind was clouded with her, his senses swamped. When he could finally see her face above his again, he knew he was lost. He was hers.

She lowered her mouth to his and whispered, "I want you now."

Gripping her hips, he pulled her beneath him and ripped away the shred of silk that separated her from him. Her face was all he could see as he rose above her. Then he pressed into her, just barely. Framing her face with his hands, he said, "Tell me you're mine."

"I'm yours," she said as she wrapped her legs around him and drew him in.

As she met him thrust for thrust, once again matching his rhythm perfectly, Jack cried out, not knowing that he called her name. Faster and deeper he raced, determined to drive her, to drive himself, higher and higher until he no longer knew where she left off and he began. Until all he knew was Corie, her scent, her taste, her body fused with his.

"Mine." He wasn't sure who said the word, only that it was spoken as they reached that final bright explosion of pleasure.

Weakened, spent, Jack had no idea how long he'd lain on top of her, trying to catch his breath, his sanity. She was trembling. So was he. But her body felt as fluid as water beneath his, and he could have lain right there forever.

When he finally managed to lever himself up, her eyes were open and on his. "I like it when you take your turn."

"Thanks. I could do it again."

He grinned then. "You'll have to give me a moment or two." Then he leaned down to brush her mouth with his. He'd meant the kiss to be gentle, not demanding. But the minute she stirred beneath him, he felt himself harden again.

"Time's up," she said against his mouth.

He thrust against her. "I guess it is." Then he let passion take control.

12

Mrs. H,

The urban legend continues to grow, and my screen-play is writing itself.

Right this minute I'm in the security offices of the Monahan House hotel, and I'm about to see the skirt trap a possible killer!

Picture the scene—my heroine, Corie, walks into the lobby bar for the meet. In moments, she will face the man who has been shooting at her. He wants his dog back.

The screen fills with a quick montage of shots—views from different angles of the security cameras in the bar. She takes a seat at the bar and orders a drink.

The camera pans the lounge. Tables are filled with shoppers finishing a late-afternoon tea and couples sipping cocktails. So far no one has approached her.

Scene shifts to the security room. Monitors on all walls provide views of the lobby, the bar, the ball-room and various hallways. Three men watch the screens—the hotel owner, the cop, and my hero, Jack Kincaid.

Corie sips her drink and glances around. No one approaches her.

The shooter is late...

Franco sighed impatiently, tucking the letter in his pocket as he moved closer to the monitor that showed the bar. "It's ten after five. No one's going near her."

"They're making her wait. It's pretty standard in these situations," D.C. said.

Jack frowned at the screen. "There's something we haven't thought of. Something..."

Jake Monahan put a hand on Jack's shoulder. "Rollo is at the entrance to the bar." He tapped a finger on the screen of the monitor. "That man sitting two stools away from her is one of my best security people. And, remember, she's wired. If something does go wrong and they find a way to take her, she'll tell us where she is. She knows what to do."

Jack glanced at his watch, then back at the screen that showed the interior of the Lewis suite. Rose Morelli stood in the living room talking to Benny.

When the two of them had arrived about an hour ago, Jake had taken them on a tour of the ballroom where the reception would be held, and for the past fifteen minutes, they'd been going over some papers in the suite. Jack had to award the older man points for acting as if everything was normal.

"Where's Buddy?" Jack asked.

"Good question," Jake said. "None of the people I have stationed at the entrances have seen him."

Jack switched his attention to the monitor that showed the bar. Corie was still sitting on a stool, holding Horatio on her lap.

Just then, Benny Lewis strolled into the bar.

"He was supposed to stay in the suite," Jack said.

Franco tapped on one of the screens. "Benny *is* in the suite."

Jack moved closer to the monitor. "Then who in the hell is that?"

"Let's see." Jake turned a knob and brought up a closer view of Corie at the bar.

CORIE WAS AWARE of the man approaching her. She'd felt his gaze on her from the moment he'd walked into the bar, but she didn't turn. Instead, she kept her attention focused on Horatio until the dog yipped.

"Ms. Benjamin?"

The sound of Benny's voice had her whirling around on the stool, and for a second all she could do was blink in surprise.

"I'm Benny Lewis."

Her thoughts raced as she grasped the hand he extended to her. Benny wasn't supposed to be here. He was to wait in the suite. That much of the plan had been explained to her.

"Do you mind if I join you?"

"No, not at all." This wasn't her father. His hands were too soft. And Benny wouldn't have called her Ms. Benjamin. Corie kept her gaze on the man as she climbed onto the stool next to her. Recognition seeped in. He was good. Buddy Lewis had not only changed his hairstyle and his clothes—he'd also changed his voice and his whole demeanor. If she hadn't met Benny the night before and talked to him, she would have been fooled by the disguise.

She waited until Buddy had ordered a drink, then said, "You came for Horatio."

He glanced down at the dog and reached out to run a hand over him. The dog licked his hand enthusiastically, but he didn't wiggle to be free the way he had last night when he'd recognized Benny.

"He doesn't usually take to women," Buddy said as he

reached for his drink. "He won't have anything to do with my sister-in-law." His hand was steady as he lifted the glass to his mouth. Then he met her eyes.

Once again, she nearly blinked. Buddy had his brother's look down pat. It was the same hard, intent stare Benny had given her when he'd first looked at her last night. Buddy Lewis was either a very good actor or he was a very different man from the one she'd seen talking to Rose at the spa.

"Let's get down to business. The real reason I asked you to come here was to tell you that you have to leave San Francisco. Tonight. I've made all the arrangements."

"Why?" she asked.

He held her with his gaze. "Because I don't want you here. I didn't want your mother and I don't want you."

Even knowing that it wasn't true of the real Benny, she was stung by his words. For a moment she couldn't speak.

Buddy reached into his pocket. Over his shoulder, she saw the man on the next bar stool tense and reach into his. It was enough to remind her that she had a job to do. When Buddy placed the envelope on the bar, she ignored it.

"That's a plane ticket back to Fairview. If you get on it, I'll set up a trust for you—two hundred and fifty thousand dollars if you agree to stay out of my life."

She lifted her chin. "You can keep the money. I'll be very happy to stay out of your life, Buddy, but I'm not staying out of Benny's."

He had the glass halfway to his lips when his hand trembled and liquid sloshed over the rim. This time when he looked at her, the hardness was gone from his eyes. In its place was fear. "You have to go before—"

"It's too late. I know that you're not Benny. You're Buddy, and you've been trying to frighten me into getting out of town ever since I got off that plane. Why?"

"SHE'S GOOD," D.C. said.

"Yeah." Jack jammed his hands into his pockets and tried to ignore the feeling in his gut that was telling him something was going to go wrong. In his opinion, Corie was too good. She must have had quite a shock when she'd first seen Buddy, but she'd held it in. And not only had she seen through the disguise, she'd also rattled him right out of his impersonation of his brother. And it was a good one. When Buddy had first spoken to her, Jack had found himself glancing back at the other monitor to assure himself that Benny was still in his suite.

"I don't have time to explain," Buddy said. "You have to leave right now and use that ticket. Your life depends on it."

All that was left of Buddy's's impersonation was the suit. The confident air he'd had when he'd entered the bar had vanished. Now, his shoulders were slumped, his hands shaking.

"He sounds scared, but it could be an act," Jack said. "He knows that plan A didn't work, so this could be plan B."

"Good point," Franco said.

Corie laid a hand on Buddy's arm. "What are you so afraid of?"

"I don't want you to be killed."

The word sent a sliver of fear sliding down Jack's spine. What if the man wasn't putting on an act?

"I'm going down there," Jack said.

D.C. laid a hand on his arm. "Give her another minute. Jake's man is only one seat away."

"You're not going to kill me," Corie said. "I've known that from the—"

"You don't understand. There's a hit man after you." As

he spoke he drew her off the bar stool. "He was at the airport that very first day. I fired the shot so that he wouldn't be able to take his. You have to leave on that plane tonight." He grabbed the ticket and pushed her toward the bar's entrance. "There's a taxi waiting in front of the hotel to take you to the airport."

"I'm not going anywhere until you tell me who wants to kill me," Corie said. "Who hired the hit man?"

"I don't think he's putting on an act," Jack said as he watched Buddy urge Corie toward the bar's entrance.

"Maybe not," D.C. said. "That would explain why witnesses described two different men at the airport."

"A second hit man?" Franco tapped a pencil on his notebook. "Who's trying to kill her?"

Jack's mind raced as the fear that had been rolling around in his stomach settled into a hard ball. Was it Benny? Had that reunion in Jake's apartment last night merely been an act? No. All of Jack's instincts argued against it. If Buddy was telling the truth, that left one other person.

On the screen, Corie and Buddy had managed half the distance to the bar's entrance when their path was blocked by a man in a paramedic's uniform. He carried a black bag and handed Corie a note. She was reading it when there was a sudden flash and smoke began to fill the screen.

"That's what we didn't think of," Jack said as he moved toward the door.

"Take the stairs," Jake said as he punched in more buttons on the board in front of him. "I'll let you know where they are as soon as I find them."

"I'll help my men cover the exits," D.C. said.

D.C.'s last words were drowned out by the deafening sound of fire alarms going off throughout the hotel.

JUST BEFORE THE SMOKE filled her vision, Corie had felt the man in the paramedic's uniform grab her wrist. Buddy had tightened his grip on her other arm. Now, her eyes were running so that she could barely see at all, but she could certainly feel the two men flanking her as they pulled and pushed her through the bar.

Benny had had a heart attack—that's what the note had said. There was a part of her that knew it was just a trick someone was using to get her out of the bar. But there was a part of her that feared something might really have happened to Benny.

Even as the panic and fear rolled through her, Corie reminded herself that the timing of Benny's possible heart attack and the fire alarm was just too convenient. She had to think. The fact that she was wired wasn't going to do Jake Monahan much good, not with the alarms deafening everyone. Screaming was definitely out, and the smoke would pretty much incapacitate the security cameras.

People bumped into them, and at one point she nearly dropped Horatio. Pressing him more tightly against her side, she felt him shiver and growl.

Rollo, she thought. He'd stationed himself outside the bar. They'd have to pass him to get into the lobby. The swinging doors they moved through were her first clue that they weren't headed toward the lobby. As she blinked the tears out of her eyes, she had time to see stainless-steel counters and a wall of refrigerators before she was pulled through a door.

Instead of taking her through another door that led to the street, the man in the paramedic's uniform urged her toward stairs. On the top step, she dug in her heels. Stall. That's what she had to do. At her side, Buddy stumbled then gripped the railing.

"Where are you taking me?" she shouted, trying to

make herself heard over the clanging of the alarms. "Benny didn't have a heart attack in the basement."

Tightening his grip on her arm, the man turned toward her, and Corie nearly shivered. His eyes were the same cold steel color as the weapon he pulled out and pressed into her side. "Benny wants to see you. He'll explain."

He was lying. Corie forced herself to take slow, even breaths as she hurried down the flight to the first landing. She had no idea how much sound would carry over the wire she was wearing. She would just have to trust that someone could hear her. Somehow Jack would figure out where they were going. Holding on to that thought, she let herself be pushed and pulled down another flight of stairs. At the bottom, the man with the gun urged her through another door.

"Why are we in the basement?" she shouted. "Where's—?"

The quick jab of the gun into her ribs cut her off. Then they were moving again, winding their way between huge boilers and sweating pipes. She'd seen the same scene in countless movies, and she tried to keep from thinking how they'd all ended.

The noise of the fire alarms ended so abruptly that, for a moment, Corie found the silence equally deafening. Rows of commercial-size washing machines lined the walls on either side of them. Sheets tumbled over the sides of carts that looked to be recently abandoned. They hurried past them. This was her chance to let them know where she was. "Why have you brought me to the laundry room? Where's Benny?"

The man with the gun jerked her to an abrupt stop. "We'll wait here for him."

THE LAUNDRY ROOM. Jack repeated the words in his mind as he felt his way through the smoke-filled bar. Jake had remained in the security room and relayed Corie's location over the walkie-talkie that Jack had pressed close to his ear. The directions were coming now—once he made it through the kitchen to the stairs that Corie and Buddy had taken, there were three more flights down and then he had to pass through the boiler room.

The first five flights, filled with fleeing hotel guests, had been the hardest to negotiate. Then he'd had to fight his way through throngs of people in the lobby to get to the lounge. The smoke here was thick, blurring his eyes and filling his lungs.

"They're still in the laundry area," Jake said into his ear. "I've got them on one of the screens. Looks like they're waiting for someone."

It couldn't be Benny. Jack would have staked his life on that. So it had to be Rose. Nearly blind, he slapped his hand into the wall, and began to feel his way to the kitchen door. He should have seen it before. He would have if he hadn't lost his objectivity when it came to Benny Lewis. He could only pray now that his mistake wouldn't cost Corie her life. Using both hands, he pushed his way through the doors to the kitchen, then paused blinking to clear his vision.

Someone crashed into him from behind, and, stumbling, Jack grabbed one of the steel tables to regain his balance. When he turned, he found himself looking at Benny Lewis.

"What are you doing here?" Jack asked.

"I was following Rose, but I lost her in the lobby. I figured something went wrong when I heard the alarm. Where's my daughter?"

"They've got her in the laundry area," Jack said. As he turned to lead the way toward the Exit sign, he noted the gun that Benny pulled out of his pocket. When he raced down the last two flights of stairs, the other man was close on his heels.

CORIE FELT LIKE she'd been standing in the laundry room of the hotel forever, but she'd counted off seconds in her head, and only about two minutes had gone by. For the first minute, she'd prayed that Jack was on his way. But for the second, she'd been trying to figure out what she could do to escape on her own.

I play it by ear. Jack's words came back to her, and for a second she felt his strength. First, she had to separate herself from her captors. The man with the gun still had a tight grip on her arm.

She concentrated on relaxing her muscles, then she sagged against him and closed her eyes. "Please, could I sit down? I feel—"

"I'll get her a chair," Buddy said.

"Don't try any tricks, old man. You've done enough to ruin my reputation," the man with the gun said. "This should have been all over at the airport."

When Corie felt the chair pressed against the back of her legs, she sank into it and bent low over her knees. She still had Horatio tucked safely against her side, but her other hand was free. Slowly, she opened her eyes. Her face was so close to her skirt that she could see the way the threads were woven. In the harsh light from overhead fluorescent tubes, they seemed to glow.

Torrie's words about the power of the skirt returned to her. If this was the same one, she might as well use any special magic that the skirt might have. Slipping her fingers beneath the hem, she rubbed the material between them and slowly raised her head.

"Don't make any sudden movements," the man said.

He had moved around to stand in front of her, and the gun was pointed directly at her.

Swallowing a bright bubble of fear, Corie continued to finger the hem of her skirt. Just doing something was giving her confidence. She watched his gaze shift to the skirt. "Don't worry. It's two against one, and I'm holding a dog."

"Make sure you hold on to it tightly. If he gets loose, I'll have to shoot him, and I don't want Benny upset tonight."

The voice had come from behind her. Corie recognized it even before she turned around and saw Rose Morelli emerge from the shadows.

"Rose, you can't do this," Buddy said, stepping forward.

"Stay right where you are," Rose said. "Or I'll have him shoot you, too."

"She's agreed to go back to Fairview," Buddy said. "I have it all arranged."

"Change of plan," Rose said as she moved closer. "I want a more final outcome this time. And since I can't trust you to handle it, I'm seeing to it myself."

"Why are you doing this?" Corie asked. A quick glance beyond Rose's shoulder convinced her that making a run for it was out of the question. The shadows and any cover they would offer were too far away. The fear rolling through her had turned into a numbing ball of ice in her stomach, and the cold was spreading through her veins at warp speed. She could barely feel her fingers. She could only hope that they were still drawing attention to the skirt—and that Jack would find her soon.

"I'm going to kill you for the same reason that I wanted to kill your mother. She was going to take away what belonged to me."

"How?" Corie asked.

"By marrying Benny. After my sister died, Benny was supposed to marry me. The house, the family, it was all supposed to be mine. It should have been mine." Her voice had become tight and hard. "Then your mother came along. Benny told me that I could still run the house, but that Isabella would take over the care of his sons. And I knew that she would eventually take over the house. I couldn't allow her to take what was mine. She had to go."

The cool dismissive tone that Rose used had the fear tightening even harder in Corie's stomach. Out of the corner of her eye, she saw that the man with the gun was still looking at her skirt, but he hadn't lowered his weapon. She had to keep Rose talking.

"What about Jack Kincaid's aunt?"

Rose laughed, and for the first time Corie heard the hint of madness. "She was a snoop, and she found out about your mother. Curiosity killed the cat."

"Rose, you won't get away with this," Buddy said. "And you haven't killed anyone yet. Let me handle it the way I—"

"Stay out of this," Rose said. "The biggest mistake I ever made was to trust you. You told me they were dead." Her voice had grown shrill, and the madness was becoming clearer and clearer in her eyes. "All these years, I believed that you'd killed them. You said that you loved me, that you would do anything for me. But you just hid them away. I wanted them dead."

"Killing is wrong, Rose," Buddy said. "You don't want to kill her."

"Yes. Yes, I do." She turned to the man next to her. "Shoot her now."

While Rose had been talking, the man had lowered the gun to his side. He didn't raise his gaze from the skirt.

"Buddy's right. You don't want to kill anyone, Rose. Neither do I. But I will if I have to."

Corie recognized Benny's voice, but she didn't turn her head. She couldn't take her eyes off the gun in the hit man's hand.

"Drop the gun," Jack said. "Corie is wired. Everything you've said has been recorded."

"No. Shoot. Shoot her." Rose screamed the words as she grabbed the gun out of the hit man's limp hand. Horatio barked and Corie felt him jump free of her hands just as Rose raised the gun and leveled it at her.

Afterward, whenever Corie replayed the scene in her mind, everything seemed to happen at once. There were shouts, but Corie couldn't make them out over the pounding of her heart. In that one split second, all she saw was Rose's face filled with fury and hatred. In the next instant, she saw nothing as Buddy stepped in front of her. Two shots rang out in quick succession and Buddy's body jerked back crashing into her. They both fell to the floor. Then all she knew was a bright explosion of pain as her head connected with the cement, and everything faded to black.

13

BENNY LEWIS definitely knew how to throw a party. From her position on the wide wooden porch of the main house, Corie had a panoramic view of the festivities. A few guests were still arriving in cars and limos. Others danced or sampled food and wine in the colorful tents that dotted the lawn. Benny was hosting the event for all of the people who had arrived at the Monahan House hotel on Friday night only to be told that the reception had been canceled. Of course the guest list had been widened to include the Monahans, Darcy and her mother, and Hawthorne and his parents. Franco had brought along Reggie, Sidney and Morgan, and Corie had just finished giving them all a tour of the house.

Although she was beginning to absorb the fact that Benny Lewis was her father, she still wasn't used to the idea that this was her home. Benny had insisted that she come here with him on Saturday morning as soon as the police had finished questioning her and the hotel doctor had checked the bump on her head and pronounced her good to go.

And that Saturday morning, a week ago, was the last time that she'd seen or spoken with Jack. She wasn't going to think about that. He was tracking down his aunt. She was happy for him, but she missed him. She glanced down at the pad she'd been doodling on for the past fifteen minutes. The whole page was filled with his name, in capital letters, in script, in gothic lettering.

She was in deep.

Turning to a fresh page, she started again, this time limiting herself to straight lines. Both Buddy and Rose had survived their bullet wounds. Benny's shot had hit Rose in the shoulder, but Rose had managed to nick Buddy's lung. After surgery, the older man had slipped in and out of consciousness for the better part of the week. The details of what had happened all those years ago to her mother and to Jack's aunt were still trickling in.

"Mind if I join you?"

Smiling, she glanced over her shoulder at her father and patted the space beside her on the step. As soon as he settled himself, he glanced at her notepad, "A triangle?"

Corie looked down at what she'd drawn. "One of those love triangles where no one is really happy. That's what it was all about, wasn't it? Buddy loved Rose, Rose loved you and you loved Bianca and then Isabella. It didn't end happily for anyone."

"That's not entirely true. I was happy with Bianca and with your mother until I lost them. And I don't think that Rose really loved anyone. She was jealous of both her sister and your mother, and then later she was jealous of Mel Kincaid when she saw that I was growing fond of her. And Buddy says that Mel had overheard something and had grown suspicious about your mother's disappearance. That's why Rose wanted Buddy to get rid of her." He looked out over the estate. "Power is what Rose really loved, and she didn't want anyone or anything to stand in her way. Left alone, she would have killed all of you. And Buddy was so besotted with her that he would have done anything for her."

"Except murder someone," Corie said.

Benny took her hand in his. "I've talked to him several times, but I don't know if we'll ever get all the specifics of how he persuaded your mother and Mel Kincaid that they had to agree to go into a so-called witness protection program. I know that he enlisted the help of some of his actor friends. We'll know more when we talk to Mel Kincaid."

"One thing we do know. He does a very effective imitation of you."

"Yes. And whatever kind of scene he staged, it was designed to convince Isabella and Mel that I had never really cut my connections to my previous associates in the east. And it was persuasive enough to convince Isabella and Mel that disappearing was their only choice if they wanted to protect you and Jack."

"Did Buddy tell you why he decided to e-mail Edie Brannigan and urge her to tell Jack about me?" Hawthorne had finally identified Buddy as Jack's anonymous e-mailer.

"He's fuzzy on that. I wonder if any of us are truly aware of why we do things. I'd like to think that he may have had an attack of conscience when he learned about your mother's death. Maybe he thought that it would be safe for you to contact me. He kept track of the both of you and sent Isabella money every year. Perhaps he was upset when Rose decided to do business with some of my old associates back East. He knew what they were capable of, and it may have been that he was worried about her. Who knows? Maybe he was finally beginning to see her for what she was."

"Did she really think she could get away with manufacturing designer drugs in your spa?" Corie asked. It had been confirmed that Dr. Mazer hadn't been making bath salts in his secret lab.

"I don't think she doubted that, even for a second. She's

a smart woman, and she'd bided her time. For the past year, I've been concentrating all my time and energy on the new winery I bought in Italy. She was banking on the fact that I would continue to travel more. And if I ever did discover what she was doing, I'm sure she felt confident that I would cover everything up for her because I wouldn't want the scandal of having a member of the family arrested on criminal charges."

"I have no doubt she was wrong about that," Corie said.

Benny tightened his grip on her hand. "Thank you."

For a moment the silence stretched between them. Then finally, Corie asked, "What will happen to Rose and Buddy?"

Benny smiled dryly. "Their lawyers are negotiating with the district attorney's office as we speak. Rose's attorneys are saying she needs treatment, and the police are still trying to figure out what to charge my brother with. He and some of his actor friends conned two people into believing that they were being taken into the witness protection program. He didn't steal money from them or profit in any way. Of course, you and Mel Kincaid could certainly file a civil suit."

"He saved my life," Corie said. "If the police let him go, what will happen to him?"

Benny put an arm around her and drew her close. "I'll make some arrangements for him. He did indeed save your life."

For a moment they sat in silence together, then Benny said, "Love is not an easy emotion, and it's never rational. I let myself believe that your mother betrayed me and ran away with a lover. I can't blame Buddy entirely for that."

"And she didn't trust you enough to ever contact you. If she'd just mailed *one* of those letters..."

He turned to her then and smiled. "There's one thing

I've learned in life. The past can't be changed. The only thing we can do anything about is the future. Have you figured out what you're going to do about Jack Kincaid?"

She shook her head. "I haven't heard from him. I know that he's looking for his aunt, but—"

"And he's found her. You'll like his aunt. I spoke with both of them a short time ago. Apparently she's tried to keep in touch with him over the years."

"Jack thought perhaps she'd been sending him anonymous fan letters."

"Sounds like Mel. I liked her a lot when she worked here, and I'm looking forward to seeing her again. Want some advice?"

Corie smiled at him. "From my father? Always."

"Time is precious. If you love Jack Kincaid, tell him so. Don't make the mistake of letting him slip away from you."

A limo pulled to a stop a short distance from the porch.

"In fact, you can tell him right now," Benny said as Jack stepped out of the limo. "I'll entertain his aunt."

JACK THOUGHT he was prepared, but when he saw Corie, the breath left his body. It was the same way he'd felt when he'd seen her in the dressing room at Macy's. Perhaps he'd known even then on some basic level that she was the only woman for him.

Well, he knew it now, and he had a plan. His aunt and Benny had both made a contribution. Benny had arranged for the limo, and his aunt had helped him pick out the ring that was burning a hole in his pocket. He was going to invite Corie for a ride, and he was going to wait until they were driving over the Golden Gate Bridge to give her the ring.

"Melanie," Benny said as he rose and walked down the

steps to meet them. "Welcome back." He drew Mel into his arms for a quick hug and then turned to Jack. "Go ahead. I'm going to steal your aunt for a while. I've had some renovations done since she left, and I want to see if she approves."

As Jack moved toward the porch, his aunt called after him, "You run along, Jack."

Jack was sure that he heard them both chuckling, but he didn't care. It had taken him six days to find his aunt, and on the plane trips to Seattle and Portland and San Diego, he'd had plenty of time to plan out what he wanted to say to Corie. And plenty of time to worry that on the roller coaster ride they'd both been on since she'd arrived in San Francisco, he'd misjudged her feelings. He had to know. He couldn't wait one more minute to find out. But as he reached the bottom of the porch steps and looked up at her, the words slipped away and fear settled in his stomach.

She looked so right standing there. This was her home now, and she had a family. She might not be interested in what he was going to offer. For the first time in his life, Jack felt his tongue loop itself into a knot.

"Hi," he managed.

"Hi."

Hadn't Franco praised him for his smooth moves when it came to women? Jack prayed for just one of them to come to mind.

"Would you like to come up on the porch?"

"The porch?" Jack glanced down to find that he had stopped at the bottom step. "Sure." Getting onto the porch would be a step in the right direction, he thought as he climbed the stairs.

"I missed you," she said simply.

Three words. He felt the rush of emotions that those words brought and wondered if he would ever get used to what she could make him feel. But it was the look in her eyes that finally loosened his tongue.

"I had a plan," he said.

"I thought you always played things by ear."

"Yeah." The fact that she was gripping her hands so tightly together that her knuckles had turned white had some of his nerves fading. "But I've changed my mind. I want to get things settled right now."

Her chin lifted, and he watched her brace herself. He very nearly reached for her then, but if he did, it might take him some time to get back to what he needed to say.

"I have something to say first," she said. "I love you, Jack Kincaid."

He did grab her then and swung her around, laughing and swearing at the same time. "Dammit. I wanted to say it first."

"Too late," she teased.

"All right." He set her on her feet, drew the box out of his pocket and opened it. "Then I'll just have to say something else."

She stared at it and then raised her eyes to meet his. What he saw there was all he wanted, all he would ever need.

"It's beautiful," she murmured.

He dropped to one knee. "Marry me, Corie."

For three long beats she said nothing.

"This isn't the time for the back-off-and-tempt plan."

"No," she said. "I just can't help but think that I'm about to break every one of my mother's commandments. I'm going to trust a charming man, I'm going to be very impulsive." She held out her hand and he slipped the ring on before he raised it to his lips. "And I'm not going to be careful what I wish for. I wish for forever with you."

A huge round of applause rose in a crescendo around them.

Still on his knee, Jack turned then and was surprised to see that a good number of people, including his aunt Mel and Benny, were watching them. Even closer, he spotted Corie's three friends from Club Nuevo. Franco had settled on the grass near the porch, notebook at the ready, and there was even a photographer from the *Chronicle* that he recognized.

Rising, he then turned back to Corie and saw laughter that mirrored his own in her eyes. "Guess neither one of us can back out of this now."

"Guess not."

"How about we give them a real show?" he asked as he drew her into his arms.

And they did.

Epilogue

September—

Mrs. H,

Picture this: late afternoon in the Napa Valley, long shadows stretch over the lawn. A montage of shots— guests sitting in rows of white chairs, a flower-covered arbor where a darkly handsome groom stands with his best man. Cut to a close-up of a string quartet—there's a swell of music as they begin to play Mendelsohn's "Wedding March." Then cut to a shot of the bride in a slim white dress, walking arm in arm with her father to where her future husband waits for her.

The music stops, and a hush falls over the assembled guests. Close-up on Benny Lewis as he places the hand of his newly discovered daughter in Jack's. Smiling, the couple turns toward the minister....

Talk about fairy-tale endings! The scene is still so fresh in my mind that I'm tearing up just writing about it. Corie and Jack's wedding took place yesterday, and that means that the skirt has now brought all three of my tenants their true loves. However, the legend continues to grow! Jack's aunt Mel wants to borrow it next. I think she's got her eye on Benny.

But let me tell you about the wedding! Torrie Monahan catered it. I finally interviewed her, by the way—more about that later! My friend Marlo at Macy's outfitted the bride and her two bridesmaids.

Corie asked Jack's aunt and Darcy to stand up with her. The groomsmen far outnumbered the bridesmaids. Jack asked his friends—Jake the hotel owner and D.C. the cop, and Hawthorne, the computer geek, while Corie asked her two half brothers plus her friends from the club. Still, they would have had a more balanced wedding party if Reggie, Morgan and Sid had worn dresses instead of tuxedos.

And the best man was none other than moi! Jack told me privately that if the skirt had anything at all to do with bringing him Corie, then he owed me for the rest of his life.

Before I tear up again, I want to give you the rest of the good news. My agent is circulating all three of my screenplays. In the meantime, she wants me to turn my three San Francisco skirt stories into an evening of one-act plays for a regional theater company just outside of L.A. But before I do that, I may take a little break and visit my mother in Savannah. Of course, I'll take the skirt with me.

The adventure continues!

Give my love to Pierre and everyone at the Willoughby!

Ta,

Franco

Is your man too good to be true?

Hot, gorgeous AND romantic?
If so, he could be a Harlequin® Blaze™ series cover model!

Our grand-prize winners will receive a trip for two to New York City to
shoot the cover of a Blaze novel, and will stay at the luxurious Plaza Hotel.
Plus, they'll receive $500 U.S. spending money!
The runner-up winners will receive $200 U.S.
to spend on a romantic dinner for two.

It's easy to enter!

In 100 words or less, tell us what makes your boyfriend or spouse a true romantic
and the perfect candidate for the cover of a Blaze novel, and include in your submission
two photos of this potential cover model.

All entries must include the written submission of the contest entrant, two photographs of the model
candidate and the Official Entry Form and Publicity Release forms completed in full and signed by
both the model candidate and the contest entrant. Harlequin, along with the experts at
Elite Model Management, will select a winner.

For photo and complete Contest details, please refer to the Official Rules on the next page. All entries
will become the property of Harlequin Enterprises Ltd. and are not returnable.

**Please visit www.blazecovermodel.com to download a copy of the Official Entry Form and
Publicity Release Form or send a request to one of the addresses below.**

Please mail your entry to: **Harlequin Blaze Cover Model Search**

In U.S.A.
P.O. Box 9069
Buffalo, NY
14269-9069

In Canada
P.O. Box 637
Fort Erie, ON
L2A 5X3

No purchase necessary. Contest open to Canadian and U.S. residents who are 18 and over.
Void where prohibited. Contest closes September 30, 2003.

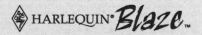

HARLEQUIN BLAZE COVER MODEL SEARCH CONTEST 3569 OFFICIAL RULES
NO PURCHASE NECESSARY TO ENTER

1. To enter, submit two (2) 4" x 6" photographs of a boyfriend or spouse (who must be 18 years of age or older) taken no later than three (3) months from the time of entry: a close-up, waist up, shirtless photograph; and a fully clothed, full-length photograph, then, tell us, in 100 words or fewer, why he should be a Harlequin Blaze cover model and how he is romantic. Your complete "entry" must include: (i) your essay, (ii) the Official Entry Form and Publicity Release Form printed below completed and signed by you (as "Entrant"), (iii) the photographs (with your hand-written name, address and phone number, and your model's name, address and phone number on the back of each photograph), and (iv) the Publicity Release Form and Photograph Representation Form printed below completed and signed by your model (as "Model"), and should be sent via first-class mail to either: Harlequin Blaze Cover Model Search Contest 3569, P.O. Box 9069, Buffalo, NY, 14269-9069, or Harlequin Blaze Cover Model Search Contest 3569, P.O. Box 637, Fort Erie, Ontario L2A 5X3. All submissions must be in English and be received no later than September 30, 2003. Limit: one entry per person, household or organization. **Purchase or acceptance of a product offer does not improve your chances of winning.** All entry requirements must be strictly adhered to for eligibility and to ensure fairness among entries.

2. Ten (10) Finalist submissions (photographs and essays) will be selected by a panel of judges consisting of members of the Harlequin editorial, marketing and public relations staff, as well as a representative from Elite Model Management (Toronto) Inc., based on the following criteria:

Aptness/Appropriateness of submitted photographs for a Harlequin Blaze cover—70%
Originality of Essay—20%
Sincerity of Essay—10%

In the event of a tie, duplicate finalists will be selected. The photographs submitted by finalists will be posted on the Harlequin website no later than November 15, 2003 (at www.blazecovermodel.com), and viewers may vote, in rank order, on their favorite(s) to assist in the panel of judges' final determination of the Grand Prize and Runner-up winning entries based on the above judging criteria. All decisions of the judges are final.

3. All entries become the property of Harlequin Enterprises Ltd. and none will be returned. Any entry may be used for future promotional purposes. Elite Model Management (Toronto) Inc. and/or its partners, subsidiaries and affiliates operating as "Elite Model Management" will have access to all entries including all personal information, and may contact any Entrant and/or Model in its sole discretion for their own business purposes. Harlequin and Elite Model Management (Toronto) Inc. are separate entities with no legal association or partnership whatsoever having no power to bind or obligate the other or create any expressed or implied obligation or responsibility on behalf of the other, such that Harlequin shall not be responsible in any way for any acts or omissions of Elite Model Management (Toronto) Inc. or its partners, subsidiaries and affiliates in connection with the Contest or otherwise and Elite Model Management shall not be responsible in any way for any acts or omissions of Harlequin or its partners, subsidiaries and affiliates in connection with the contest or otherwise.

4. All Entrants and Models must be residents of the U.S. or Canada, be 18 years of age or older, and have no prior criminal convictions. The contest is not open to any Model that is a professional model and/or actor in any capacity at the time of the entry. Contest void wherever prohibited by law; all applicable laws and regulations apply. Any litigation within the Province of Quebec regarding the conduct or organization of a publicity contest may be submitted to the Régie des alcools, des courses et des jeux for a ruling, and any litigation regarding the awarding of a prize may be submitted to the Régie only for the purpose of helping the parties reach a settlement. Employees and immediate family members of Harlequin Enterprises Ltd., D.L. Blair, Inc., Elite Model Management (Toronto) Inc. and their parents, affiliates, subsidiaries and all other agencies, entities and persons connected with the use, marketing or conduct of this Contest are not eligible to enter. Acceptance of any prize offered constitutes permission to use Entrants' and Models' names, essay submissions, photographs or other likenesses for the purposes of advertising, trade, publication and promotion on behalf of Harlequin Enterprises Ltd., its parent, affiliates, subsidiaries, assigns and other authorized entities involved in the judging and promotion of the contest without further compensation to any Entrant or Model, unless prohibited by law.

5. Finalists will be determined no later than October 30, 2003. Prize Winners will be determined no later than January 31, 2004. Grand Prize Winners (consisting of winning Entrant and Model) will be required to sign and return Affidavit of Eligibility/Release of Liability and Model Release forms within thirty (30) days of notification. Non-compliance with this requirement and within the specified time period will result in disqualification and an alternate will be selected. Any prize notification returned as undeliverable will result in the awarding of the prize to an alternate set of winners. All travelers (or parent/legal guardian of a minor) must execute the Affidavit of Eligibility/Release of Liability prior to ticketing and must possess required travel documents (e.g. valid photo ID) where applicable. Travel dates specified by Sponsor but no later than May 30, 2004.

6. Prizes: One (1) Grand Prize—the opportunity for the Model to appear on the cover of a paperback book from the Harlequin Blaze series, and a 3 day/2 night trip for two (Entrant and Model) to New York, NY for the photo shoot of Model which includes round-trip coach air transportation from the commercial airport nearest the winning Entrant's home to New York, NY, (or, in lieu of air transportation, $100 cash payable to Entrant and Model, if the winning Entrant's home is within 250 miles of New York, NY), hotel accommodations (double occupancy) at the Plaza Hotel and $500 cash spending money payable to Entrant and Model, (approximate prize value: $8,000), and one (1) Runner-up Prize of $200 cash payable to Entrant and Model for a romantic dinner for two (approximate prize value: $200). Prizes are valued in U.S. currency. Prizes consist of only those items listed as part of the prize. No substitution of prize(s) permitted by winners. All prizes are awarded jointly to the Entrant and Model of the winning entries, and are not severable - prizes and obligations may not be assigned or transferred. Any change to the Entrant and/or Model of the winning entries will result in disqualification and an alternate will be selected. Taxes on prize are the sole responsibility of winners. Any and all expenses and/or items not specifically described as part of the prize are the sole responsibility of winners. Harlequin Enterprises Ltd. and D.L. Blair, Inc., their parents, affiliates, and subsidiaries are not responsible for errors in printing of Contest entries and/or game pieces. No responsibility is assumed for lost, stolen, late, illegible, incomplete, inaccurate, non-delivered, postage due or misdirected mail or entries. In the event of printing or other errors which may result in unintended prize values or duplication of prizes, all affected game pieces or entries shall be null and void.

7. Winners will be notified by mail. For winners' list (available after March 31, 2004), send a self-addressed, stamped envelope to: Harlequin Blaze Cover Model Search Contest 3569 Winners, P.O. Box 4200, Blair, NE 68009-4200, or refer to the Harlequin website (at www.blazecovermodel.com).

Contest sponsored by Harlequin Enterprises Ltd., P.O. Box 9042, Buffalo, NY 14269-9042.

HBCVRMODEL2

HARLEQUIN®
Temptation.

AMERICAN HEROES

**These men are heroes—
strong, fearless...
And impossible to resist!**

**Join bestselling authors Lori Foster, Donna Kauffman
and Jill Shalvis as they deliver up**

MEN OF COURAGE

**Harlequin anthology
May 2003**

Followed by *American Heroes* miniseries
in Harlequin Temptation

**RILEY by Lori Foster
June 2003**

**SEAN by Donna Kauffman
July 2003**

**LUKE by Jill Shalvis
August 2003**

Don't miss this sexy new miniseries by some of
Temptation's hottest authors!

Available at your favorite retail outlet.

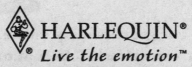

HARLEQUIN®
Live the emotion™

Visit us at www.eHarlequin.com

If you enjoyed what you just read,
then we've got an offer you can't resist!

Take 2 bestselling love stories FREE!

Plus get a FREE surprise gift!

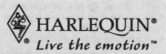

Blaze ™

◆ HARLEQUIN® *Blaze* ™

Rory Carmichael is a good girl, trying to survive the suburbs.
Micki Carmichael is a bad girl, trying to survive the streets.
Both are about to receive an invitation
they won't be able to refuse....

INVITATIONS TO SEDUCTION

Enjoy this Blazing duo by fan favorite
Julie Elizabeth Leto:

#92—LOOKING FOR TROUBLE
June 2003

#100—UP TO NO GOOD
August 2003

And don't forget to pick up

INVITATIONS TO SEDUCTION

the 2003 Blaze collection
by Vicki Lewis Thompson,
Carly Phillips and Janelle Denison
Available July 2003

Summers can't get any hotter than this!

◆ HARLEQUIN®
® *Live the emotion* ™

Visit us at www.eHarlequin.com

HBJEL

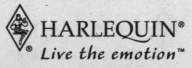